DEATH OMEGA STATION

A BEYOND THE CRADLE NOVELLA

JOHN L. FRENCH

eBooks
Pennsville, NJ

PUBLISHED BY
eSpec Books LLC
Danielle McPhail, Publisher
PO Box 242,
Pennsville, New Jersey 08070
www.especbooks.com

Copyright © 2025 John L. French

ISBN: 978-1-956463-37-8
ISBN (eBook): 978-1-956463-36-1

All rights reserved. No part of the contents of this book may be reproduced or transmitted in any form or by any means without the written permission of the publisher.

All persons, places, and events in this book are fictitious and any resemblance to actual persons, places, or events is purely coincidental.

Copyediting: Greg Schauer and Danielle McPhail
Cover and Interior Design: Danielle McPhail, McP Digital Graphics

Images - www.shutterstock.com

Cover:
View from a porthole of space station on the Earth background © Paopano
Blood collection © Gluiki

Dedicated to the memories of

Steve Silvia, a friend I never met

and

Ronald Hullock, the first friend I ever made

Cast of Characters

THE ANASI
Del Caprine — Ambassador to Omega Station

THE DAGON
Jebe — Ambassador to Omega Station

THE HUNTA
Herat — Ambassador to Omega Station
Bocaj — Herat's former assistant
Walid — Herat's Assistant
Loy — Adrian Cray's partner
Nomis — A physician

THE KARP
Subedi — Ambassador to Omega Station
Ekim — Hired muscle
Lorac — Aide to Subedi

THE PREADA
Olubek — Ambassador to Omega Station
Exios — Docking Bay Worker
Ivalie - Chief of Maintenance
Elandra — Friend of Dominick Grimes

THE TERRANS
Adrian Cray — Detective/Truth Finder, Terran Investigative Service.
Victor Flandry — Ambassador to Omega Station
Dominic Grimes — Assistant to Victor Flandry
Sheila Murphy — Aide to Victor Flandry

Prologue

Herat walked toward his suite, inwardly fuming after another fruitless meeting. *Fools,* he thought, *how did they expect to get anything accomplished with an even number of members on the council? The Preada are food and had no right >to a seat. True, they are intelligent after a fashion and have their uses, but we Hunta are dominant on Sauros. But no, thanks to the Karp they have a voice. And we should never have admitted the Terrans. What intelligent race kills their own kind for petty reasons?*

I need to kill something.

Herat's mood darkened as he realized that there was nothing to kill. It had been that way for some time now.

"With respect, ambassador," his aide Bocaj had nervously told him some weeks before, "we must stop. The others are beginning to notice."

"Notice what?" Herat asked so sharply that Bocaj tucked his tail and lowered his head in submission. "They are the underclass—workers, servants, and there are over two thousand of them. A few should not be missed."

"Among their own kind they are. They talk among themselves, and like smoke, their words rise to higher levels. I've made arrangements. An FTL is arriving from Sauros next week. It will have what you need."

"Alive?"

"Somewhat drugged, but alive. And young. It will suffice until those missing have been forgotten."

"And the others?"

"Like us, they will have to wait."

"How long?"

"A few months, then we can resume."

"Very well. When we do, any chance of getting a Terran?"

"Not as yet. Remember what Ambassador Subedi said about them."

"Thank you, Bocaj. You may go."

The aide carefully backed out, relieved that Herat had not taken out his anger on him. But then, only Terrans kill their own. Well, the Karp do, but they have a reason. *Still*, Bocaj reflected, *things change*.

But there had been no young Preada on the next ship, or the one after that. Only frozen meat. Herat thought to have a word with Bocaj but then remembered that his former aide was now in Maintenance. Herat was not yet sure of the new one, Walid. She seemed too honest, too rigid.

Maybe if I offered to share?

He put this out of his mind and decided to shower, the meeting room had been cold, and he needed to warm his body. Then he'd dine in the station mess. He'd order his meat rare and sit close enough to the Preada so they could watch him eat and remember how it was.

The thought lightened his mood. So much so that when he entered his suite, at first he failed to notice the presence of another.

"What are you doing here?"

Before he could get his answer, Herat was seized from behind and his head pulled back to expose his throat. His survival reflexes were slow to react and by the time his claws finally came out, something very sharp cut deep into his neck. He shuddered once and was still, his lungs emptying themselves of air.

Sure of their kill, the assailant released the body. Pausing to make sure the way was clear, they left as silently and unseen as they had arrived, leaving Herat to die alone on the floor of the greeting area, his green blood staining its yellow carpet.

Chapter One

The FTL shook as the winds of the Ackley Field buffeted it. It had been that way since I left Terra for Omega Station, but these were the strongest winds yet. A murmur from my IMplant told me that the AI-Pilot was correcting course.

The winds were not supposed to exist. When first discovered as a practical means of cheating the speed of light, the Field was static. What we called "wind" was a disturbance in the Field that started about ten years ago. Ships of other races had been lost, believed to have been blown off-course. No Terran ships though. Our navigational AI was better, based as it was on the global positioning systems of the late-twentieth century. When we began interstellar flight, we used them rather than trust the skills of Terran pilots. AIs may be crap when it comes to the creative arts or scientific reasoning, but they know how to get from point A to point B, whether the two points are on Terra or in the enormity of space. Being the newest members of the Collective and needing to get back into the others' good graces after the Anasi Affair, we provided the other races of the Collective with the appropriate technology, which was almost immediately improved upon by the Preada of Sauros. The Preada are very good at improving other races' technology, now that they no longer have to worry about being eaten by the Hunta, the other sophontic race on Sauros.

Since then, only one FTL had been lost in the past two years, but that was a Dagon ship, one not equipped with the Terran/Preada Interstellar Positional System. The Dagons are a secretive race, one that is suspicious of any tech they did not develop. But after the loss of their ship, they finally "allowed" the installation of the IPS in their vessels.

Still, the Ackley winds kept growing stronger, creating the possibility that an extremely strong wind could severely damage an FTL or blow it too far off course to recover.

Why that was, no one in the Collective knew for sure. The prevailing theory was that FTLs created ripples as they traveled through the Field. These ripples became the Ackley Winds. The more FTLs, the stronger and more frequent the winds.

<Course correction made,> the AI-Pilot whispered in my head through my IMplant. It then informed me that instead of being almost there, it was now about eight hours to Omega Station. We Terrans call it Omega not because it's the last of its kind but because it's shaped like the Greek letter. I don't know what the other races call it. It doesn't matter, with one exception it's not like we can understand each other. (There's always an exception. I think it's some kind of rule.)

Omega was discovered by the Karp. It appears to have been abandoned by a race believed to be extinct and, according to the Karp, is at least 500 years old.

Omega Station hangs in interstellar space. How it's powered no one knows. The station's physical plant is located on the lower level of each arm. To date, none of the races wants to explore too far into it for fear of pushing the wrong button, flipping the wrong switch, or triggering something the (hopefully) extinct race left behind that would cause the station to explode with all hands on board. Of course, one day it could do that anyway. It's not something anyone wants to think about.

The station is "home" to over 3000 sophonts from the six known races, most of which are support staff. The others are researchers, scientists, and engineers. It's perfect for astronomers and astrophysicists. I'm told there are even a few astrologists on board, working together to develop a universal theory of how the stars affect us.

And, God help us, there are the diplomats.

Being neutral ground, it is the perfect place for representatives of the Collective to meet to discuss, and hopefully resolve, problems that affect them all. Like whether to intervene when a killer asteroid is about to destroy a planet on which there is non-spacefaring sophontic life. That vote has been taken on three separate occasions. The first two went four-to-one against interfering.

< Fewer problems for us should they one day develop an FTL drive,> Ambassador Subedi of Karp was reported as saying prior to the first vote to allow a planet of sophonts to die.

<*It is the dark gods' will,*> agreed Ambassador Jebe of Dagos.

And so a planet died. And then another.

This changed after Terra, having discovered the Ackley Field on its own, was invited to join the Collective.

"Think of it not as saving another race," the Terran ambassador Victor Flandry said. "Instead think of it as practice for when one of our worlds is threatened." The motion to save the water world we Terrans called (what else) "Atlantis" passed by a vote of four to two.

"Very good," Flandry said, proud of his first success as a member of the Collective Council. Then he threw it away by adding, "If some of you can develop a delivery system, Terra will supply the nuclear bombs."

The room went silent as the other five races struggled to understand the implications of what their IMplant translation apps told them Flandry had just said. That Terra, alone among the races of the Collective, had weaponized the processes of fission and fusion.

The idea that one race of the Collective had the power to rain horrible death upon the others scared the hell out of them. That and the Anansi Affair left them wondering whether inviting Terra to join the Collective had been a good idea.

As for the Anasi Affair. The Anansi resemble Terran spiders except that they're the size of ponies. Two years after their arrival on Terra, Abel Cooper, a detective with the then Eath-United Investigative Service, was sent to Anansi to investigate a murder committed at the Terran Legation, the first ever murder on an extra-Terran planet. It was a simple case which he solved quickly. The aftermath, however, almost led to interstellar war. On learning that Terrans kill each other for reasons other than war, ritual, or honor, the Anasi decided we were a threat to sophonts everywhere and tried to destroy us with biological weapons. The result was such a hilarious failure that we Terrans did not even bother to retaliate. But it only added to our dangerous reputation among the other races. In the words of Subedi:

<*They kill their own for no reason. They build weapons that can destroy their planet. They are crazy and dangerous. Let us not fuck with them.*>

Actually, the word Subedi used was a lot more vulgar in that it is almost taboo in their culture, only used when great emphasis is required.

The current problem was that of the Ackley Winds. If a solution could not be found and the Field became too unstable to navigate, then interstellar travel might cease and each of the known races would once again be alone in space.

But aside from the fact that I was a member of one of those races and if space travel shut down I'd miss visiting other worlds, that was not my problem. Mine was more direct. The murder of Ambassador Herat.

Chapter Two

The Ackley Winds were on the Collective Council's agenda the day it was discovered that someone had given Herat a second mouth. The issue was whether or not to construct heavier FTLs that might better withstand the winds. Some were concerned that heavier ships would cause a greater disturbance in the Ackley Field and thus stronger winds.

Three of the ambassadors were in favor of the construction—Herat, Victor Flandry, and Subedi. Against the proposal were the other three ambassadors—Jebe of Dagos, Del Caprine of Anasi, and Olubek who, like Herat, was from Sauros. Sauros had two representatives because it had two sophontic races. Olubek was a Preada. Not so long ago, the Hunta hunted the Preada as game animals. They don't anymore but a nasty Hunta pejorative for Preada is literally "food."

The Hunta are a proud race. To be late for, or worse, fail to attend a meeting is considered disgraceful behavior. As a result, Herat was always the first to arrive, casting his reptilian eye at the others as they came in. (Knowing this, Olubek was always the last to arrive, frequently a few minutes late.)

All but Herat had assembled in the meeting room. It was unlike the ultra-punctual Herat not to be there. After some minutes, Jebe suggested sending Walid, Herat's aide, to check on him.

<*Maybe he is ill?*> they said to the others.

<*Wait,*> said Del Caprine of Anasi. <*Remember what he did to the last aide to interrupt him.*> Del Caprine twisted her upper torso to look at the aide. <*I like Walid. I would not want her exiled to Maintenance.*>

The aide nodded her reptile-like head and parted her lips just enough to show teeth. A Hunta's smile. <*Thank you.*>

<I'll go,> Del Caprine said. <He will be angry or embarrassed, but I do not think he would roar at an ambassador. And if he does, I'll bite him.>

There was a general chuckle at this, with each of the ambassadors expressing their amusement in their own way.

De Caprine rose from the couch on which she'd been reclining and skittered toward the residential section, her six legs clicking on the hardwood floors as she did.

About fifteen minutes later, the ambassadors' IMplants all but screamed, <COME AT ONCE TO HERAT'S SUITE!>

When they arrived, they found Del Caprine standing outside Herat's open door. <It opened at my touch,> she said. <When it did I saw...>

She pointed into the suite.

One by one they looked in and saw the lifeless body of Ambassador Herat on the floor of the greeting area of his suite, his throat a gaping wound.

<What do we do?> asked Subedi.

As one they looked at Victor Flandry. He was the Terran ambassador. As a Terran, he was most likely to be familiar with the kind of death that Herat's open throat suggested.

"Call a physician. Have them examine Herat to formally determine that he's dead. When that is done, each of you choose one of your most trusted people to form an... honor guard outside his door, letting no one in, not even his own kind. And then..."

Del Caprine interrupted. <We have to call a Truth-Finder.>

And that's where I came in.

I was one of those Truth-Finders Del Caprine had mentioned. On Terra, we're called detectives, but I have to admit "Truth-Finder" is a better term.

After the Anansi Affair, the other races became fascinated with Terran Truth-Finders. They all had people who could solve problems but the fact that there were sophonts who, on their own, could solve unsolvable problems using logic, imagination, and intuition amazed them. Highly-trained Truth-Finders became one of Terra's most sought-after exports. But not for murder. Not until now.

At the time of the Anasi Affair, there was no way to transmit information through the Ackley Field. Messages had to be sent on an FTL. Since then, a team of scientists on board Omega developed a method of instantaneous transmission using quantum phenomena. So on the same day that Herat's body was found, I drew the short straw and was soon outbound to Omega. What should have been a three-day trip lasted a week thanks to the Ackley Winds. Every time my FTL shook I prayed to God, then, once the ship was back on course, thanked Them, the Terran team that had developed the AI-pilot, and the Preada who had improved it.

I used the extra time to relax, catch up on my reading and VR videos, and of course, review the case and the sophonts involved.

I mentioned the Anansi, spiders the size of ponies. When we first met them, they were friendly and funny, chuckling at the cute spider names we gave them. (Shelob, Peter, Parker, Charlotte, you get the idea.) Once they tried to wipe us out using the small, furry creatures that were the males of their species, the jokes didn't seem funny anymore.

Think of the velociraptors of Terra's Late Cretaceous period, that's sort of what the Hunta of Sauros look like, only they're feathered and when standing fully erect are about seven feet tall, Mostly they crouch, which brings them down to six feet. The males have bright plumage and sport crests. The females don't have a crest and their feathers are duller.

The other Sauros are the Preada. They're short bi-pedal mammals that, to a Terran, resemble a mix between an otter and a raccoon. The raccoon part comes from facial markings that look like masks. Females have light-colored fur, males are darker.

The Karp look nothing like fish. Don't ask me where the name comes from because I don't know. In appearance, they resemble Terrans except their bodies bear stripes and swirls of various colors. Despite being the first of the known space-faring races to have discovered the Ackley Field, their culture is feudal in nature and somewhat Victorian.

Then there are the Dagon. All capes, hoods, tentacles, and spooky as hell.

In addition to the quick exobiology lesson, there were audio and video recordings of a few council meetings that Ambassador Flandry had provided. There was, of course, a recording of the one that broke up when Herat's body was found. There was also the one before that when the vote on the heavier FTLs was taken as well and the one that came after the body's discovery during which a reluctant Walid was voted in as "acting head" of the Hunta legation. The vote was four-to-one, the nay being cast by Olubek. He argued that he should represent all of Sauros. The others disagreed.

I didn't have much to go on. There was no surveillance outside or within the ambassadorial suites. Valuing their privacy, none of the races of the Collective felt the need for it. As the last invited to the party, the Terrans decided that installing cameras outside their quarters might insult the others.

So the only independent footage taken before the murder being discovered was that from inside the conference room.

I did have the crime scene footage Flandry insisted on having taken. I watched it once or twice. It didn't help. I'd have to do my own search then process the scene and the knife for physical evidence. And, of course, question those involved.

Chapter Three

My arrival at Omega Station was uneventful. With no planetary atmosphere to worry about, the AI-pilot left the Ackley Field just fifteen minutes out from the station. The AI guided the FTL to Omega's outer curve and put it gently into a third-level docking bay. There I was greeted by a uniformed Preada who had dark fur, a white mask, and was wearing blue coveralls with the Omega symbol on it.

<Welcome to the Station of the Collective, Truth-Finder Adrian Cray. I am Exios,> he said. His spoken voice was very pleasant and made me wish we didn't have to speak through my translation app. Maybe one day.

<May I scan you for hazardous materials and/or dangerous weapons?>

As rainbow lights washed over me, I was tempted to ask Exios what use a non-dangerous weapon would be and if everyone was checked for them or just the "dangerous" Terrans. But he was just a working stiff and didn't need my smartassery. I decided to save that for those in charge.

< Ambassador Flandry has been waiting for you. Do you want me to advise him of your arrival?>

What I wanted was to listen to Exios talk for another twenty minutes or so. As I said, the Preada are mammals and I found myself wondering if Exios liked dangerous, Terran males who stood six-foot tall and weighed about 90 kilos. After reminding myself that I was on duty and would be until I found the killer I said,

"Thank you, Exios, but may I be shown to my quarters? As close to the ambassadorial suites as possible. I would like to rest before viewing the crime scene. Oh, and if possible, I would like an adjacent suite in which to work."

<*Of course, Truth-Finder. Your request for rooms was sent ahead, as were your dietary preferences. Is there anything else you... desire?*>

Lord! Are all the Preada like this or does this one just have a thing for Terrans, I asked myself. Then I wondered if he was a spy.

"No, thank you. If I need anything I'll let someone know."

<*Will you require an aide, Truth-Finder?*>

It would be helpful, but an aide might also be a spy. "No, thank you."

Exios escorted me to my suites. If he was hoping I would invite him in he was disappointed. Not that I have any moral objections to relations with compatible, consenting sophonts but as I said, I was on duty.

I had requested two suites, one of which I planned to use as my office. They each consisted of a sitting room equipped with a more than decent entertainment system, a bedroom, and a spare room. The latter had a table and a desk on which was an AI-Tablet. Standard equipment apparently, but for security's sake I decided to use my own. I also scanned both suites for surveillance devices. (There were none.) Each suite had a small bathroom and an even smaller kitchen. That last didn't concern me. I would be taking most of my meals in Omega's mess. With my IMplant properly adjusted, it would be the best place to catch at least some of the station gossip.

I thought about taking a nap. Then thought about trying out the entertainment system. But I'd done too much of both en route, so I decided it was time to do what I was being paid to do.

But then my IMplant advised me of an incoming call. Ambassador Flandry. Having already set up my AI-Tablet, I transferred the call to that.

I knew from the info provided to me that Flandry was in his mid-fifties. He was about five-seven with thinning blond hair. His weight was not provided but that doesn't matter so much in space where your weight changes depending on where you are. I always felt that the important thing was keeping fit.

Flandry looked fit, and officious. He scowled at me as he said,

"Detective Cray, I would like to know why you did not report to me upon your arrival."

Oh, I thought, *he's going to be a fun one*. I lost no time in setting him straight.

"Let me make one thing clear, Ambassador Flandry. I am an agent working for the Terran Investigative Service, which has assigned me to investigate the suspicious death of Ambassador Herat of Sauros. I do not work for you and so I do not report to you."

"Still, Cray, as a matter of courtesy, you should have…"

"Courtesy is one thing, Flandry, appearances are another. The other races of the Collective don't trust us much if at all. How would it look if, as soon as I arrived, I had a private chat with one of the suspects in this matter?"

Flandry started sputtering. "Sus… suspect. How dare you, why I…"

"Until I clear them, everyone is a suspect. Now then, I have recorded this conversation, and it will be part of my final report. Please do not contact me again unless you have information pertinent to the case being investigated. I will send you a message when it's time for your interview."

"What interview?"

"Standard procedure, ambassador. All suspects must be interviewed. I'll be collecting evidence from you at that time as well. Cray out."

Chapter Four

The ambassadorial suites were on the first (top) level of Omega. Not only were there accommodations for the Collective Council but their aides also had rooms, although not as large as the ambassadors'. Each suite was customized to meet the needs of those using it.

Atmosphere was not a problem. The Collective was "O_2 breathers only." I don't know if any non-oxygen breathing sophonts had been discovered but if they had, they were probably told to form their own club.

For the Anansi, the beds had been replaced with floor-level cushions. The Karp always requested extra-large beds, since they seldom slept alone and more than two was common. There were no beds or cushions in the Hunta suites. They rested standing up, balancing on their tails. Some had chairs for their non-Hunta guests. The kitchen refrigerators and cooking devices had a wide range of settings that could be adjusted for what was being cooked and how.

My quarters were not formally a part of the ambassadorial wing, but they were a close walk. When I got to the ambassadorial section, the Omega Central AI recognized that I had access and admitted me. I had also been granted access to Ambassador Herat's suite. In fact, at my request, I was the only one who did have access.

A Hunta was standing just outside the door to Herat's suite, the first I'd seen other than for vids and images. This one was just slightly taller than me and had bright red feathers and a crest to match. A male then.

He was at attention, standing upright with his tail erect. From the impression in the carpet behind him, I suspected he had been resting on it and only snapped-to when the passageway door opened.

On seeing me, the Hunta raised his left hand and extended his claws. With my left hand mimicking claws, I did the same. A greeting of equals.

<I am Loy. Are you Truth-Finder Cray?> I said that I was. <You have come to honor Herat by finding out how he died?>

Loy was wearing a black uniform tunic and kilt. (Trousers are not practical when you have a tail. The Hunta kilts are cut to allow for them.) Loy's voice was harsh, all hisses and low growls. When I replied, "I am, both how and why," I wondered how I sounded to him.

<Then my duty as Honor Guard is done.>

There was some relief in his voice at being finished with a noble but boring job.

"Before you leave, I must ask if anyone has tried to gain entry."

<Do you see any blood on the floor, walls, or ceiling?>

"No, I don't."

<Then no one has tried to enter.> The guard then gave me the same smile I had seen Walid make. I smiled back. We exchanged salutes and he left.

Del Caprine had reported that the door to the suite had opened to her touch. My examination before entering showed no signs of force. Did Herat admit his slayer? Did the slayer have their own access? Was the door left unlocked? Or did a third party remotely unlock it? This left me wondering how easy it would be to hack into Omega Central and if it recorded comings and goings.

At my request, Omega Central opened the door and, after putting on gloves and disposable shoe covers, I went in.

The suite was much like mine, although Herat's had smaller sleeping quarters and the spare room was large enough for meetings. Unlike my quarters, this one had two shower stalls, one considerably larger than the other.

Other than the bloodstain evidence where Herat's body was found, the greeting area looked undisturbed. There was art on the wall and figures and other objects on two small tables. All this was intact. So were the two visitor chairs. So unless the killer was overly neat, there had not been a struggle.

Herat's body was not there. Flandry had it removed to a freezer unit pending my examination. There was a knife next to the stain where Herat had lain. It was a large one, a killing knife, of the type used by the Karp in their honor duels or by us Terrans, for whom such a knife has many purposes, including killing those we do not like. The Hunta sometime use such a knife to butcher their kills when they don't want to get their claws messy.

From the knife's size and shape, I initially ruled out the Anasi. While historically they have no problem with killing other races—remember, they tried that with us—I didn't think they could grip that large a knife with what they use for hands. The Preada could though. I could imagine one of them using it as payback for centuries of being hunted. Although at five-foot they'd have to stand on a chair to do the deed. (And then put it back.) But I couldn't picture a Hunta allowing a Preada into their quarters, unless they had invited one to dinner. (Bad joke, Adrian. Stop that.) I reserved judgment on the Dagons until I learned more about their tentacles.

Nothing else appeared disturbed. Nothing ransacked, nothing searched, nothing disturbed. The killer wanted only one thing. Herat's life. They took that and left.

Chapter Five

I got to work. Starting with both sides of the door, then continuing into the suite I used a multiphasic scanner to search for contact points and body fluids. Whether you're Terran or not, Locard's Theory still applies. If you enter or leave a crime scene, you're going to leave something behind and/or take something away. So I scanned for sucker marks (Dagons), tactile adhesive (Anansi), and friction ridges (the rest of us.) My search also included looking for, well, let's call it GenSeq (genetic sequences) since the races used different kinds of polynucleotide helices to turn more than one set of genetic material into a new, singular creation. Given what little I knew about Dagon biology, I wondered how many helices their GenSeq contained. I also wondered if it would be impolite to ask. It didn't matter, I'd find out when I collected prints and samples.

There was a considerable amount of GenSeq. Not uncommon in well-used living quarters. I'd have to eliminate Herat's, Walid's, and the aide who was exiled to Maintenance. Being a suspicious sort, I was curious to see what kind of GenSeq turned up.

The scanner indicated that it had located and recorded some ridge detail and adhesive but nothing that it considered sucker marks. The adhesive I would have to collect to see if came from an Anansi. The knife I packaged so I could examine it more closely in my suite. After releasing a micro-drone to take overhead scans of the suite, I began the laborious task of collecting GenSeq samples and vacuuming every surface of the suite for trace evidence.

All this took several hours. Not that I noticed. On a crime scene, you don't think about the time, only the job.

One more walkthrough of the suite and I was done. Knowing I'd probably have to go back, when I left I instructed Omega Central to secure the door and open it only for me. I also instructed it to alert me if anyone other than me tried to enter.

After finishing in Herat's quarters, there was one more thing to do before it was back to my suite and some much-needed rest.

After leaving the ambassadorial section, I secured all that I recovered in an evidence box in my suite then headed for the medical bay. Loy was waiting for me in the corridor outside my quarters.

<It occurred to me, Truth-Finder, that whatever you learned in and removed from Herat's quarters will tell you who killed him and maybe why.>

"I'm hoping it will, Loy. And please, call me Cray."

<Thank you, Friend Cray. I fear that whoever killed Herat might try to harm or kill you to keep the truth from coming out. To honor Herat, I will guard you.>

Another possible spy? I asked myself. Or was this the mystery novel scenario where the killer volunteers to help the detective? Who knew? But my cop sense told me Loy was legit and I had to trust someone. Besides, I'd need a Hunta to operate Herat's tablet, which was not made for Terran hands.

"Then you honor me as well, Friend Loy."

There are no lifts or stairs on Omega, just gently sloping ramps from one level to another, with bridges linking the two arms. The bridges are strong transparent structures and the brightest engineers of five planets have yet to figure out what they're made of.

The medical section was one floor down on this side of the station. At first, we walked the ramps in silence. Halfway down, Loy asked, <What will happen to the killer when you find them?>

"That won't be up to me, Loy. My job is to find them. Their fate will be determined by the Collective Council."

<And if the killer is a member of the council?>

This was a sensitive subject. Still, I saw no reason not to tell him.

"Maybe nothing. They might have diplomatic immunity."

<Not from me they won't.>

"I didn't hear that, Loy. Sometimes these translator apps don't work too well."

Loy's grunt told me that we had understood each other very well.

Loy led me to the large sick bay, where physicians of five worlds treated their own races and learned how to treat those from other worlds.

The Hunta physician was Nomis. A foot shorter than Loy with dull blue feathers and no crest. She was wearing gloves and the largest surgical mask I'd ever seen.

<You are Truth-Finder Cray?> I said that I was. <And this is?>

"This is Loy. He is with me as friend and protector."

Nomis's eyes narrowed almost to slits as she looked first at Loy then at me. Then she tilted her head to the right. (That's how Huntas nodded.)

<As it should be. Now, get dressed. Truth-Finder, your PPE is over there.>

Once gowned, Nomis led us over to Herat. He was on an examination table that was designed to accommodate his tail. His feathers were a mixture of white and red. His plume, which I imagined once stood tall and proud, was deflated in death. His body was covered from the waist down.

"Any wounds or other concerns on his lower body, doctor?"

<No. And Herat's toxicology came back normal.>

"Forgive my asking, doctor, but it is my job to do so. Did you test for non-Hunta drugs or other substances?"

No nod this time. Just a slight circling of her head.

<You will have the report on those results tomorrow. I will send you the results I do have.>

"And the cause of death?"

<Is obvious. Exsanguination due to Herat's throat being cut.>

"Thank you, doctor." I moved closer to the body. "May I?" When Nomis nodded, I lifted Herat's neck and looked at the wound. I motioned for my bag. When Loy brought it, I took out my scanner and ran it over his neck and shoulders as well as the wound. I made a note to compare the wound to the knife.

I stepped back. Replacing my scanner, I checked my IMplant. Nomis had sent her first report.

"Thank you, doctor. I'm done here but please retain the body in case other examinations are required. I look forward to receiving your supplemental report. Oh, one more thing, Doctor Nomis."

<What is that, Truth-Finder?>

"Does the Medical Section keep records of station personnel?"

<Of course.>

Do those records include the personnel's GenSeqs?"

<No, why would they?>

To make my life easier, I thought. "To help in identification in case of a multiple-victim accident."

<That would be impractical. Besides, on arrival, all station personal are equipped with sub-cutaneous identification. Sub-cuts are easier than having to replace lost ID cards.>

"Are these sub-cut trackable?"

< I do not know about the tracking, but they are scannable, and records are kept of their usage. You will see in my report that Herat was identified by his sub-cut.>

"Okay, thank you, doctor."

Loy insisted on escorting me back to my quarters. On the way,

<She did not check for non-Hunta material, did she?>

"I don't think so, but she covered up well."

<I would not have thought of that either. That is why you are the Truth-Finder.>

When we got to my quarters, I asked Loy to step inside. "I need your help." He was glad to give it.

Once in the greeting area. "Loy, can you act as if your claws are extended?"

<Yes.>

I got behind him. "I'm going to attack you. Please respond normally but without the claws."

<Very well.>

Without any further comment or warning, I stepped behind Loy. With one hand I grabbed his head and pulled it back to expose his throat. Thanks to the size and shape of his head it was easier than I thought. As I did so, Loy's hands came up in an attempt to rake my hand and arm with his imaginary claws. But my other hand, the one with the "knife" in it was across his throat before he could. I released him.

"Thank you, Loy."

<It was a pleasure being attacked by you, Friend Cray. I will leave you to your work and see you tomorrow.>

I had no doubt he would.

Loy was right about the work. I started the scanner downloading what I had recorded. Then I read Nomis's report.

In addition to confirming the cause of death, she had preserved the clothing he was wearing when he was found in case I wanted to examine it. (*I should have asked about that,* I thought. Well, that made up for Nomis not doing a full drug screen.) Since Herat had died with his claws extended, she examined them but found no "foreign material."

Nomis also included a detailed description of Herat's fatal wound. It was enough to initially consider the knife I recovered from the crime scene as the murder weapon. Initially. Nothing is anything unless confirmed. I entered the scan I had made of the knife and instructed the AI-Tablet to compare the knife to the autopsy results. Having done all I could do; it was time to rest.

Chapter Six

As it often happens when I'm on a job, my sleep was troubled. Some dreams were of being buffeted forever by Ackley Winds in an FTL that was slowly falling to pieces. Others of walking a crime scene that went forever in both directions. Where were the flying dreams I had as a child? Or the more interesting ones of my adolescence? I think I slept peacefully maybe one hour of the three that I allotted myself.

Breakfast was no more a joy than my sleep. The food was good, North American Terran fare—French toast, Belgium waffles, Canadian bacon, and some non-national treats. But I ate my food and drank my milk and orange juice alone. The mess had an open floor plan—anyone could sit anywhere. But as if to show that "human nature" is not limited to Terrans, members of each race tended to sit and eat together. But that could have been the food. After all, what smells good to one race might disgust another.

But I sat alone. No Terrans came near me. None of the others either. Well, one did. Loy followed me from my quarters to the mess, not making contact but pretending we happened to be going the same way. He did not eat near me either but was close enough that if trouble broke out, he could get to it before it got to me.

I understood. I was the stranger in their midst. The outsider hunting one of their own and maybe with a hidden agenda. And if any were seen talking to me, maybe they were informing.

It was Loy who made the first move. Picking up his tray, he walked over to my table.

<Friend Cray, may I join you?>

"Friend Loy, I would be honored."

<The honor is mine.>

Looking at my breakfast, Loy asked what I was eating. He didn't care about the waffles or toast but was quite interested in the bacon.

<What kind of an animal is a Canadian?>

I explained the true nature of the food and offered him a slice. He took it gladly, enjoyed it, and offered me a bit of his breakfast.

<Don't worry,> he said. <You didn't know him.> Fortunately my translation app added <old Hunta joke> so I laughed appreciatively.

<It is a type of deer,> he explained. <My people no longer eat Preada. At least, most of us don't.>

I was glad he had said it. I was worried how and if I should broach the subject with him. Before I could comment, he went on.

<We do eat a non-sophontic subspecies that the Preada raise. At least, that's what the little ones... forgive me, the Preada, tell us. They could, of course, be lying. Perhaps they are improving their race by sending us the slower, weaker, and less intelligent of their kind. But that's their business. Not mine.>

We then got off the subject. Ignoring the stares of those around us, we told each other about our home planets, our "earths" if you will.

Breakfast finished, it was time to work, me to my quarters, Loy to his security duties. Then I had an idea. Exios had asked if I needed an aide. Why not Loy?

<I would be pleased and honored, Friend Cray.>

I put in a request with Omega Central and Walid. Given my status, it was more of a demand, and Loy was assigned to me for the duration. He could stay in my extra suite for his comfort and my convenience.

"You don't mind, do you?"

<Not at all. My cabinmate snores.>

We walked back to our quarters together, attracting stares and quietly daring anyone to do anything about it.

We had a full day ahead of us. I spent the first part of it letting Loy know all that I had done to date.

"Have to keep my new partner informed."

<Partner?>

"Cops don't have aides," I told him. "They have partners."

<What's the difference?>

"Partners work twice as hard. Now, I want you to review the microdrone footage of the crime scene."

<What am I looking for?>

"If I told you, you'd only look for that. Just review it and let me know what you think."

I removed the surveillance software from the AI-Tablet that had been left for me, cloned it with mine, and gave it to Loy to use. I also made sure that if he tried to send information to anyone but me I'd know about it. While he watched the drone scans, I began on the knife, scanning it for touch marks (friction ridges, sucker marks, and contact adhesive) and swabs for GenSeq. While I did that, I set the GenSeq analyzer to work on the crime scene swabs.

<I would not have thought this possible.>

Loy may have only been thinking out loud, but I've programmed my translation app to pick up even the slightest vocalizations and whisper them into my inner ear. A handy thing for any detective to have.

"What was possible, Loy?"

<It's just that... Friend Cray, how much do you know about Sauros?>

"Not much," I admitted. "Your planet is one large continent. It comprises two-thirds of the planet and is dotted with lakes, rivers, and the like. The remainder of the planet is water. The Preada live on one side of the continent and your people live on the other.

<Yes. Because of a very large, almost impassable mountain range that runs the length of our continent, we were unaware of each other's existence. During our age of discovery, ships sailed west, and aircraft flew over the mountains. When we found the Preada we thought they were simply intelligent animals and well, hunted them for food and their hides. We soon discovered that further inland was a civilization as advanced as our own, although in different ways. They captured our ships and aircraft, improved them, and waged war on us. And this war continued for centuries until the Karp came from space and, well, some say intervened, and others interfered. They offered us the stars if the wars ended and the Hunta stopped eating the Preada.>

"Let me guess. Not everyone accepted that."

<No, they did not. It embarrasses me to say that there is still a black market in Preada flesh and even private hunting preserves.>

"Loy, I wish I could tell you that Terrans were better, only the truth is, we were far worse. But that is a topic for another time. Anyway, tell me, what has all this to do with what you saw in Herat's suite?"

Loy shifted the view to the bathroom. <This larger stall. Do you know what this is?>

"No."

<It is called a butchering room. It has no purpose other than for a Hunta to kill live game and devour it raw.>

"And?"

<*The importation of live animals, whether as food or companions, is not permitted onboard this station. Herat must have installed the butchering room himself.>

"How often is it cleaned?"

<*It is not. It is said that the odor of past food enhances the taste of the current meal.>

I had taken a swab of every stain I found in Herat's suite. It had been a matter of routine and I had been tempted to restrict myself to the immediate scene. After listening to Loy, I was glad I had been thorough.

Call it "cop instinct." I had a bad feeling about this butchering room. But until the GenSeq results came back that's all it was, a feeling. Still, I decided to get the "what-if" ball rolling.

"Loy, I'm going to start scheduling individual interviews with all those who have access to the ambassadorial suites."

<*As your partner, how can I help?>

"Try to find out how many sophonts of every race have been reported missing or cannot be accounted for since Herat arrived."

<*You want me to hunt for people who are no longer here?> The way Loy put it sounded silly until he said, <*Sounds like fun.>

While Loy went about his ghost hunt, I spent my time making appointments. I decided to start with the ambassadors and work my way down if necessary. Of the six, five of them were "too busy" to be individually interviewed by a Truth-Finder and took "great objection" to being considered suspects in Herat's death. Four of them pointed out that since murder was a particular Terran trait I should look in the direction of the Terrans and leave the rest of them alone. The exception to the last was, of course, Victor Flandry who wanted to know why I hadn't solved the murder yet and why I had engaged "one of them" as an assistant when he would have willingly detailed one of his staff. I declined to answer either question but did make a note to suggest in my final report that he might not be the best person to represent Terra.

The one exception to all this was Walid.

<*Truth-Finder Cray, as acting Ambassador of the Hunta Legation, I see it as my duty to cooperate with you fully to discover who butchered Herat, why they did it, and repay them in kind.>

"I appreciate that, Acting Ambassador Walid. Just keep in mind that my job is to find the who and why. The final disposition will be with the council as a whole, but I'm sure that as Herat's successor, your views will be given great weight."

She seemed satisfied. As for the others, after egos were smoothed and veiled threats made, I had a full slate of interviews scheduled over the next two days. As it turned out, well, best-laid plans and all that.

Loy soon came to me with the results of his hunt. His head was bobbing and his mouth open. This told me that he was well pleased with what he had found.

<Ambassador Herat arrived three years ago as part of the original Hunta delegation. He was the primary assistant to Sibanu, the original ambassador. When Sibanu returned to Sauros, she appointed Herat as her successor. That was two years ago. He has been in place ever since.>

A word about time. Given that there are five planets, each with its own annual revolutions and four with daily rotations (Dagos is tidally locked), each race measures time in its own way. And then there is Omega time. My app translates everything to Terran time.

"Assuming there were disappearances, when did they begin?"

<Roughly two months after Herat's promotion, right after he appointed Bocaj primary assistant.>

"How many?"

<Discounting those who may have deserted by stowing away on departing FTLs, there are forty-one possible disappearances. I determined this by accessing the sub-cut IDs of station personnel. Forty-one are off-line. >

"How many of these were reported?"

<None, there is no station command to whom to report.>

I don't know how long I stared at Loy in sheer disbelief before asking him, "You mean there is *no one* in charge of the station?"

<Why would there be? The central AI runs the station autonomously according to the hardware and software that was present when the Karp discovered it. Duties are AI-assigned and shared among the races. A workers' council arbitrates disputes. There are, of course, guards and security to handle troublemakers. Offenders get locked up for a time. Repeat offenders are placed on the next outbound FTL, regardless of destination. >

"Forty-one sophonts missing and no one noticed?"

Loy gave a very Terran-like shrug. <Their fellow workers probably assumed that they had been reassigned. As for those in charge, let me ask you, Friend Cray. On Terra, do those in charge ever notice or even care about what happens to those who do the work?>

He had a point. "How many missing by race?"

<No Hunta. No humans. No Dagons. Some Anansi and Karp. The rest Preada.>

That bad feeling I had about the butchering room got worse. Something told me that the GenSeq results would only confirm my worst fears.

<My translator is telling me you look worried, Friend Cray. Why?>

If Loy was going to be my partner it was time for him to learn what it was like to be a cop.

"Let's check the GenSeq results. Then we'll talk."

As I said before, I had taken a lot of swabs. I downloaded the results to our AI-Tablets and sorted them by location and race. Then I pulled up the results from the butchering room.

It was as Loy had said — No Hunta GenSeq other than Herat, Walid, and Bocaj, no Terran, no Dagon. The rest was a mixture of some Anasi and Karp with the majority Preada. The problem was that I had only taken thirty-two samples from the butchering room.

I watched Loy read the results and waited for him to realize what they meant. He made a noise that my app told me was akin to a sob. And if you've ever wondered if Hunta can cry, well, they're as human as anyone else.

<This means...>

"Yes, it does."

<But why? And why not...>

"Herat would not kill his own. And I guess he remembered Subedi's advice concerning Terrans. An offensive Hunta word for Preada is 'food.' I guess it was more than a word to Herat. As for the rest of the samples, I guess he liked variety in his diet."

<There are forty-one sophonts presumed missing. You recovered and analyzed thirty-two samples. While you may have missed a few, you could not have missed all nine.>

"I hope not. I'll have to teach you how to swab for samples and you can double-check me. But you're right. More sophonts are missing than we can account for. It looks like Herat was not the only one enjoying forbidden fruit."

<But the ones eaten were meat.>

"Sorry. It's a Terran expression for something taboo."

Loy gave his version of a nod and again looked at the results. Then he looked at me. The only thing I could think of telling him was what my old partner told me the first time I looked into the Abyss.

"Who knows what evils lurk in the hearts of sophonts? Cops do. I do. Now you do. Welcome to the Job."

Loy stood.

No more sobs. No more tears. Only a look of determination.

<*What's next?*>

"The Council needs to be informed. And later we'll have to see how well Omega Central tracks the sub-cut IDs. Right now, I'm going to review the rest of the GenSeq results."

I could tell Loy was itching to do more than computer work.

"Tonight after dinner we'll pay a visit to Maintenance to find Bocaj and see what he has to say about his former employer."

Chapter Seven

As I requested, Loy arrived at the mess in his uniform black tunic and kilt. "Bring a weapon if you have one," I told him. He smiled at me and replied, <*I don't need one,*> and flashed his claws. I dressed in something official-looking. Red shirt, black cargo pants, black jacket. Not having claws, I brought a weapon. More than one, actually.

Again we ate alone, unless you count the stares. We got plenty of them. It's not unusual for the different races to mix socially. The scientists and the support staff do. They work together so why not eat together, drink together, and… well, one can get lonely when they're on a space station far from home, lonely and curious. Use your imagination.

But Loy and I were different. No one wants to get too close to hunters on the prowl.

Loy had his usual meal of "someone I did not know." Although that joke's not funny anymore. After seeing the results from the butchering room, I had no appetite for meat. Fortunately, the head chef must have been an Italian cook because I enjoyed a very nice spinach lasagna.

There were maintenance stations on each level of each arm. Not knowing exactly where Bocaj was assigned, Loy and I headed for the main office, which was on the fourth level of the other arm.

<*There are shuttles that travel the arms,*> Loy told me. (I was wondering what those long golfcart-type things were.) <*But I think you would appreciate going through a passage tube, at least once.*>

The passage tubes connected the arms. There was one on each level. We walked down to the fourth level and crossed over.

Loy was right. Crossing the tube was fantastic. While the flooring was opaque, the upper walls and top were transparent, displaying the wonder of space as it is rarely seen. From your planet, you take a shuttle to an orbital station. The FTL launches from there. There are no stars in the Ackley Field and no windows on an FTL. But inside the tubes, all of creation is open to you. Arthur C. Clarke had it right when he wrote, "My God, it's full of stars."

How long I stood and stared I don't know. I do know that Loy tugged on my arm too soon.

<We must go now, Friend Cray. The stars are always there, and will wait for us.>

"How do you…"

<I keep my eyes down and my head straight or else I become as lost as you.>

As we walked the tube we passed others as lost in the rapture of nearly open space as I was. But there were not as many as I thought there'd be. I guess you can get used to anything.

"What does this Bocaj look like?"

< His feathers are dark green and brown, and he has a small lighter green crest. He is a little taller than me. He is bigger all around but probably soft from the easy ambassadorial life. This maintenance job must be painful for him, both from the work and the humiliation. I meant to ask, why are we questioning Bocaj? It would not be like one Hunta to kill another.>

Which is why, I said to myself, Herat did not kill Bocaj. Assuming he did not arrange for someone in Maintenance to do the job for him. To Loy I said,

"When Truth-Finders are on a job, they often expose more than one truth. Herat's 'dining habits' may have led to his death. Bocaj likely knew about them, maybe even received Herat's leavings."

<Why do you say that?>

"Friend Loy, you have been my partner for less than two days and you have learned things no one but me knows. Think about how long Bocaj was with Herat. How much do you think he knows? Maybe enough to tell us who else was involved. And who may have had reason to kill him."

<But Hunta would not kill Hunta.>

"Maybe, maybe not. We Terrans can be very bad influences. And other races may have been involved. Maybe some of them enjoy 'forbidden fruit' as well. They may not eat their own, but they might like the taste of some of the others."

<Who knows what evil?> Loy said quietly. <We too have a saying. The more you stare at the Devil the more it looks at you.>

"And yet we stare, Friend Loy, because the Devil knows the Truth, and it is our job to make it tell us."

The fourth level on each arm was used mainly for storage, shipping and receiving cargo, and station stores. When we finally left the passage tube, I saw people coming and going, each one about their own business. It took me longer than it should have to realize that no Terrans were among them. No Dagons either.

"Friend Loy, where are the…"

<Dagons? Terrans? The Dagons are too solitary. They do not like to mix. And their presence disturbs others. Terrans have not been here long enough. As the station grows, there will be a need for more workers. Perhaps the station recruiters will go to Terra. They will promise a new life on a new 'world' that has new opportunities When the workers arrive, they will discover the same life, no real opportunity, and that one world is much the same as any other, no matter how it is made.>

It was a walk to the office. As the only Terran there, I felt more strange than I did in the mess. Everyone we passed stared at Loy and me, knowing from our dress, our walk, and our attitude we did not belong and had not come for any good reason.

The door to the office suite was marked by a sigil that our apps translated as <Maintenance – official business only> Since we were as official as it comes, we knocked once then went in.

A Preada met us. She looked me up and down and spared a quick glance at the Hunta beside me, not showing any fear or concern. This Preada's fur was almost white. Her mask face was black, and her coveralls were red and labeled Chief of Maintenance.

<I am Ivalie. You should have called. You should not have come here.>

That voice. Ivalie's natural voice had the same pleasant, seductive timbre as did Exios's. Remembering my encounter with him, I asked myself if they were all like that. Shaking off the effects of Ivalie's voice, I threw a look at Loy and nodded my head, indicating that he should take the lead.

<Yet we are here, and we would like some information.>

When a Preada frowns their mask crinkles. <Send a request through the proper channels.>

I waited to see how Loy would handle being defied by a member of a race that his had once hunted for food. Did he have an instinctual desire to hurt, kill, and eat this small sophont? Now that he had been, albeit temporarily, entrusted with the power of the law would he act the bully?

Calmly but with authority, he replied, <This is Truth-Finder Cray. I am Loy, his partner. We are the proper channels. Consider the request sent.>

Ivalie did not respond. She just stood there, staring past Loy and toward me. I'm not good at reading other races' expressions, but hers looked to me as if she was sending a message to someone via her IMplant. Finally,

<What do you want to know?>

Loy looked at me. Again I nodded. This was his show. I wanted to see how he did.

<We are looking for Bocaj of Hunta. He was assigned to your section not long ago.>

Again there was that pause before Ivalie replied. It made me wonder who she might be sending to and if there was a way of hacking into someone's IMplant.

Ivalie smiled. <Yes. I know him. A severe demotion, the almost high brought low.> Another pause. This time she was checking Bocaj's schedule. <He is on the second level of this arm scrubbing communal toilets, at least one of which has been reported clogged.> A shrug, which seems a universal gesture. <What can you do? Is there anything else? If not, there is a ramp not far from here. Turn left. And next time, Hunta, have the courtesy to call first.>

<This was us being courteous, Ivalie of Preada. The next time we will simply summon you and if you do not respond, we will... find you.>

We left. As we walked to the ramp I said, "You did well, Friend Loy. Very well. But tell me, you almost said 'hunt' didn't you?"

<It had occurred to me, but I did not want to do her the honor of threatening her.>

"Do they all have that kind of voice?"

<The very pleasant, very seductive voice?> I nodded. <Only when they "are in the mood," or so I'm told. It does not affect us, only other mammals. I am also told that they are not fussy about who they mate with. Are you...>

Loy did not have to finish the question.

"One rule of cop work, Friend Loy. Do not mess with anyone who might be a suspect. And right now, everyone on this station but you and me are suspects."

<Too bad you are not my type, Friend Cray.> There was that Hunta smile again. I guess cop humor comes naturally.

We were on the ramp leading from the third level to the second when they came for us. I figured Ivalie or whoever she had messaged must have sent them. There were four of them. Two had been waiting for us, two were coming up from behind. The last two were Preada, both with rust-colored fur. Twins maybe. They held some kind of clubs. Of the other two, one was a Hunta, with black and white feathers in a striped pattern and a poor excuse for a crest. The last, judging by their striped face, was a Karp. The Karp wasn't armed. The Hunta had his claws out.

<Start recording.> I told my IMplant.

"You should not have come here. Now we have to hurt you," the Karp said in passable Terran. Being physically close to Terrans, with a similar body structure and vocal cords, many of the Karp have learned to speak Terran.

"Yet, we are here." I figured if the Karp could copy Ivalie I could echo Loy. I decided that this was not the time or place to hold a rational discussion. So did Loy as we stood back-to-back, Loy facing the Preada. "Take them, Loy."

As Loy described it later, he got into a hunter's crouch and unsheathed his claws. With his crest rising as high as it could, he said something like, <Looks like dinner's come early,> and let out a roar that bounced off the rampway's walls. That was all it took because the two Preada peed themselves and ran down the ramp as fast as they could.

I had to take his word for that because I was busy with the Hunta and Karp. Before they could approach, I took out my baton and fully extended it.

"Is that all you have? A stick against me and one of the Collective's deadliest hunters?"

That called for a quip or two but I didn't have the time. The Hunta crouched as Loy must have and came at me. Sharp teeth and claws, lots of power, no real training. I ducked beneath his claws, thrust my baton into his midsection, and hit the button that turned on the juice.

I had studied Hunta physiology. I knew just how many volts would kill one. I gave my attacker just a little less than that. There was screaming and jerking and a bad odor as the Hunta fouled himself.

That left the Karp. Seeing he was outnumbered two-to-one, he tried to retreat up the ramp. So I hit him with my baton (no juice) and he went down.

With Loy watching over the still-twitching Hunta, I approached the Karp.

"Name," I demanded, pointing my now sparking baton at his tender parts. I knew his were similar to Terrans' so I was betting they'd hurt in the same way.

<Ekim,> he said, shifting back to his own language.

"Who?"

I moved my sparking baton closer enough so his bits would feel the electricity. Loy enhanced things with a low growl.

<It was Ivalie. She told me you were intruders and to take care of them, eh, you.>

"She didn't tell you we were Truth-Finders?"

<That *** didn't even tell me one of you was Terran.>

Whatever Ekim called Ivalie was not translatable. I assumed it was not a compliment.

<What are you going to do with us?>

<We don't have time to deal with scavengers.> Loy said. Scavenger is the ultimate Hunta insult. It refers to a Hunta who does not hunt but follows the pack to eat its leavings.

"Do not go back to Ivalie. We will know if you do. Let her worry. She is not your friend. We will deal with her. Now take this one and go."

Ekim grabbed the Hunta under the shoulders and pulled him down the ramp. We continued upward.

<Are we reporting this?>

"To the Collective? Eventually. But for now let's find and talk to Bocaj."

<He may not be there. Ivalie might have warned him.>

"So we pay another visit to Ivalie and ask her where he is. If she won't tell us, we'll ask her to step outside."

<But that would... oh, I see. But why would she believe you?>

"Because I'm Terran, and everyone knows we're all crazy and violent. But I don't think Ivalie warned him. She probably thought the not-too-fantastic-four would stop us."

<They may have been a decoy to slow us down while she sent another hunting party to make sure Bocaj didn't talk.>

"Then we better hurry up."

Chapter Eight

We found Bocaj where Ivalie told us he'd be, in a second-level bathroom. He wasn't exactly cleaning it. Instead, he was washing the inside of the bowl used by most of the races with his snout, aided by one of his fellow Hunta and a Karp. There was a flush then the Hunta said,

<We'll ask you again, scavenger. Why were the Truth-Finders asking about you?>

<I've told you, I don't know.>

"Why don't you ask us?"

Our intrusion surprised Bocaj's assailants. I was able to get behind the Hunta. I had her head back and my shock rod sparking against her throat before she could release Bocaj. When she did let him go I said, "If you move or your claws come out, you get the full dose. I wonder what burnt Hunta flesh smells like."

The Hunta tucked her tail and would have lowered her head if I didn't have a good hold on it.

While I was taking care of the Hunta, Loy grabbed the Karp and slammed her several times into the porcelain that seems to be universal throughout the Collective in decorating bathroom walls. And yes, once we had everything under control I checked the walls and the stalls. Graffiti in five different languages.

But that was after Bocaj tried to make a break for it. He didn't get far. Loy whipped around and tripped him with his tail.

<So what do we do with him?> Loy asked as I was cuffing Bocaj.

"We call a shuttle and take him back to your suite. The workroom there will serve to question him."

<And if he doesn't answer?>

"Your suite has a bathroom. We can always try drowning him."

<I like your out-the-airlock idea better.>

The questioning of Bocaj did not take long. My questioning, that is. Loy just stood there looking menacing, his claws out and a spare, sparking shock rod in his hands. Unlike Terran criminals, those of other races have no experience with police interrogation techniques, whether learned from books, vids, or practical experience.

At first, Bocaj did not believe Herat was dead, much less murdered. We had to show him the stills.

<It wasn't me!>

"I don't care. Herat got what he deserved." Then I told him about the GenSeqs found in the butchering room.

"If I checked, would I find your GenSeq among the slaughtered. How did it work? You did the slaughtering in exchange for a taste of off-world meat?

<No, no, it wasn't like that.>

"So Herat did the butchering himself?"

<Yes! Eh, no!>

"Yes, no. So who was it, you or him?"

<It was him. I only, only...>

"Only what?" As if he realized he'd already said too much, Bocaj stayed silent.

"There are two ways this can play out. This first is that this was all your doing. You arranged it all—the abductions, the butchering, the sharing with others. Herat went along because he was weak. You were the Hunta, he was the scavenger. When he finally regained his courage and was going to expose you, you played the Terran and killed him."

<But I was in maintenance.>

"All the better to find victims. What do you think, Loy, what would be a just punishment for such a... monster?"

<Deliver him to the Preada and tell them what he's done. Then give them all knives and tell them they have safe passage with him for three hours.>

We had rehearsed the above, in case I could get us this far. Loy wasn't happy with it, but he went along once I assured him it was all part of the interrogation technique.

It worked. Bocaj took the implied out.

<You said there were two ways.>

"You were the scavenger, doing Herat's bidding, and you ate some of the forbidden meat because he ordered you to, so you couldn't betray him. When it became clear you couldn't or wouldn't help him anymore, he sent you to Maintenance knowing you'd have to keep quiet."

<*That one!*>

They almost always take the out.

"Loy, get your tablet and start recording. Bocaj, we're going to need times, places, and names. Names of the FTL pilots involved, names of the sophonts on the station, Hunta and otherwise, who shared the meat, the ones who procured the meat, and, if possible, the names of the victims."

Bocaj gave it all up. He had a wonderful memory and told us what he knew. As for what he didn't know, he gave us the names of those who did.

This was going to cause a station-wide mess involving a massive clean-up effort. So I alerted the members of the Collective Council that I was calling an emergency assembly and gave them a meeting time.

Reactions were mixed. Most seemed pleased, assuming that Herat's murder had been solved. Some wanted to know the details right away. Subedi and Flandry both assumed that the one-on-one interviews had been canceled.

"No, they haven't been canceled. Just pushed back. This is a more serious matter. I'll explain at the meeting." I logged off. Loy and I tied Bocaj so he couldn't move. (Actually, Loy did the tying, I watched so I would know how to firmly secure a Hunta if the need arose. It turns out the tail is the tricky part.)

I took the first watch. Loy went to sleep. Bocaj did too, which left me free to do some work.

The results of the analysis of the knife had come back. No identifiable contact marks. Not surprisingly, the knife's hilt was rough, all the better to grip with. The GenSeq swabs came back positive for Herat on both the blade and the hilt. No surprise there, it was found near his body. You would expect there to be traces of his blood on both. You'd also expect to find his skin cells on the edge of the blade. There were none. Not an impossible result but an unlikely one. The hilt also had its surprises. When swabbing it, I encountered a sticky substance. Blood, I thought. Blood, even when dried, can be slightly sticky. So can the adhesive that the Anasi uses to grip things. And that's what the results from the GenSeq swab of the hilt told me it was.

I had initially dismissed the possibility of an Anasi cutting Herat's throat because one hand would not be able to do it and I could not imagine Herat remaining still for a two-handed cut. But now the evidence suggested otherwise. And while it might be misinterpreted, the evidence never lies.

A daring swashbuckler move, a frontal, two-handed assault? No, Herat would have seen her coming, unsheathed his claws, and would have had to explain a dead Anasi in his suite. Maybe not, he might have just eaten her. This thought reminded me to ask Loy what was done with the inedible parts. Then I remembered the disposal unit in the kitchen. Anything not wanted and no longer useful goes down the chute and into the fire that powers the great beast Omega.

Bocaj started to stir so I set aside thinking for guarding. When he was conscious, he forgot where he was and that he was bound and almost toppled over. But he righted himself, which was a good thing for him because I was just going to leave him where he fell.

Once he was steady, I said,

"All right, Bocaj, listen up. Loy's asleep. It's just you and me in here. The recorders are off." (I lie about other things too.) "There are things I need to know to understand this whole thing."

<What?>

"First off, how does Preada taste?"

After all that he had told us, it was a reasonable question. Maybe he thought I was considering trying some myself. If I let it slip that I was, it would give him a hold on me. So he answered.

<Not bad. But the meat from the herd animals we raise for ourselves tastes better. So does that stuff the Preada supply us with but not by much.>

"And Anasi and Karp?"

<Anasi's good but you have to be careful how you fix them, so the poison doesn't get you. As for Karp, it depends on how you cook them. The private parts are the best.>

"Ever had any Dagons?"

Bocaj shuddered and let out an untranslatable oath. <Are you kidding? Would you put those things in your mouth?>

"So if safer, tastier food is available, why take the chance and eat sophonts?"

Bocaj didn't reply so I answered for him.

"It's a domination thing, isn't it? Once upon a time, the Hunta were the only intelligent race. Then you found the Preada. Then the Karp found you. Then there were us Terrans and the Anasi. Your people went from being the alphas of creation to just one in a crowd. So you eat the flesh of the others to show you're more powerful than them."

Bocaj nodded. <*Yeah, Herat said something like that. That's why he supplied the others. To show them they were no better than us. Sometimes, he'd feed them their own and tell them it was some other race.*>

"How do Terrans taste?"

<*Never had any, but I wouldn't mind a taste.*>

"Had Herat?"

<*I don't think so. But he had applied for a position at our embassy on Terra.*>

That would have been fun. Terrans disappearing, detectives figuring out who was causing it but unable to do anything because of diplomatic immunity. Finally, some unofficial justice that would either be hushed up or turned into an interplanetary incident.

Bocaj had had a long and strenuous day and began to doze off. I was close behind him and might have nodded off, but Loy came in to relieve me.

I think I got an hour's sleep. Dreams of a huge feast in which everyone was served to one another. Someone asked about Terrans and was told to wait for desert. Then an Anasi (I think it was Del Caprine) grabbed a carving knife and turned a Hunta into the main course.

That woke me up. I remember saying, "There is no way she could have survived," which brought me back to the problem I was working on before Bocaj woke up.

An Anasi could not have attacked Herat from behind, and she would not have survived a frontal assault. Impossible but the evidence said otherwise. But what was that Bocaj said?

<*Anasi's good but you have to be careful how you fix them so the poison doesn't get you.*>

Then I remembered the video of the meeting that took place right before Herat's body was found, the one in which Del Caprine said,

<*…And if he does, I'll bite him.*>

I checked my IMplant in-box. Dr. Nomis had sent her follow-up report. I had just been too busy to notice. I sent a belated "Thank you" and began to read it.

The report noted that a foreign (i.e. non-Hunta) substance was found in the second tox screen. It was a fast-acting poison that the Anasi used to paralyze their prey before devouring it. The poison is harmless to Terrans, they found that out when they used it in an attempt to kill the legation personnel. No one knows its effects on other races but, given Hunta body chemistry, the poison might not kill him, but it might knock him out or at least slow him down.

So I pictured the killer somehow getting the poison into Herat, waiting for him to collapse, then slitting his throat. The killer drops the knife and waits for the body to be found.

Or more likely, they drop *a* knife but not the murder weapon. Remember, there were no skin cells on the blade.

Tired, I drifted off to sleep. This time my dreams were a rabbit hole of possibilities of how and why Herat was killed. The last was my favorite in which the rest of the Collective Council were involved in his death because they could no longer stand his always being on time.

Chapter Nine

The meeting with the Collective Council went as I expected. Except for Walid and Jebe, none of the others appeared happy to be there. Walid was taller than the average Hunta female, with dull yellow feathers. She seemed genuinely interested in our investigation of her predecessor's death As for Jebe, between the cloak, hood, and the tentacles, who knows what a Dagon is thinking?

Flandry started the fun. When I greeted the council members with, "Thank you all for coming," he replied, "It's not like we had a choice."

"You did have a choice, Ambassador Flandry. You could have refused to come. Of course, your refusal would have been recorded for the record."

"You mean, I'd be marked absent like in school."

"Well, you are here to learn something."

I do not know how this was translated to the other members, but it did get the equivalent of a chuckle out of them, again, except for Jebe. I think. Maybe a certain pattern of tentacles means laughter.

I had Loy wait just outside the conference room with the door cracked open so he could hear. After my "pleasant" exchange with Flandry, I called out, "Bring him in, Loy."

Loy walked in with Bocaj in tow. And I do mean "in tow." Bocaj's feet were shackled. His hands were tied tightly in front of him, and his tail lashed to his body. According to Loy, this method of binding meant that the Hunta in question was in disgrace, that he was no longer a member of the pack. Worse yet, Loy led Bocaj using a rope tied to his wrists. Until he was unbound, Bocaj was merely cattle.

"What the hell are they doing here?"

Why does the hothead in the group always have to be Terran? Or maybe it was just Flandry? In my dream, the other ambassadors conspired to murder Herat. In real life, I think they'd be likely to kill Flandry. Not only that, I would probably help them. I think The Powers-That-Be on Terra may have sent Flandry to Omega Station to be rid of him. They probably held a farewell party right after his FTL left the Sol System.

"The bound Hunta is Bocaj, Herat's former assistant. The other is Loy, my partner in my investigation and apprentice Truth-Finder."

"Who approved that?"

Walid answered for me. <*I did. A Hunta was... killed. It seemed only fitting that a Hunta help find the truth of his death. Truth-Finder Cray, I trust there is a reason you have Bocaj bound like an animal?*>

"I do, Acting Ambassador Walid."

<*I am no longer acting, Truth-Finder. I was informed just before this meeting that I have been promoted to Herat's position.*>

"Congratulations, ambassador."

<*Congratulations are not necessary. No one else wanted the job. To be so far from my world, so far from my pack. It is not what I wished. But you said there was a reason for your humiliation of Bocaj.*>

"There is, ambassador. And once I have explained what I have found, I will release him into your custody and leave his fate in your hands."

I shifted my attention and addressed them all. "Members of the Collective Council, I came to Omega Station to find the truth about Ambassador Herat's death, why he was killed, and who killed him. This much you know. An investigation into the truth is like a journey." (I almost said "hunt" but at the last minute I realized that Olubek might take offense.)

"When you start on a journey, you have a destination in mind. But along the way, another path emerges that you must take. And so you detour. Such is the case now."

Then I threw the grenade into their midst. I told them about the butchering room and the GenSeq swabs I took from it. I told them that the swabs came back as Karp and Anansi but mostly Preada. I then had Loy tell them how he discovered that forty-one station workers could not be accounted for.

These were intelligent sophonts, even Flandry. They quickly realized the implications of what I had told them and began to stare suspiciously at Walid. Seeing she was about to object I shook my head. She got the message and stayed silent.

"But theories require proof before they become fact."

I told them about Maintenance Chief Ivalie and how she had sent a mix of sophonts to take care of us. And I told them how I found two more rigorously questioning Bocaj and how we took him into custody.

"Forgive me, Truth-Finder," Subedi said in passable Terran, probably just to show he could speak it, "But as you said, theories require proof. Where is the proof of what you have implied."

"And what have I implied, Ambassador Subedi?"

We all knew what that was, but I wanted one of them to say it.

Having shown off, Subedi switched to his native tongue. <*That Herat and possibly others were abducting, slaughtering, and devouring members of other races. But I ask again, where is your proof?*>

"Loy, if you would?"

Loy had brought his tablet. He pressed play and the video of Bocaj's confession appeared on the wall. The ambassadors watched in stunned silence as it played out. When it was over, I played my late-night conversation with Bocaj, the one I had told him I was not making.

It was Jebe who broke the silence.

<*I am somewhat insulted that the Dagon are not considered suitable for consumption. From time to time, we shed our limbs and grow new ones. We devour our shed limbs among ourselves and with those of other pods. We find ourselves very delicious. Truth-Finders Cray and Loy, we would be honored if you would join us at our next communion.*>

"The honor would be ours, Ambassador Jebe. Perhaps after all the truth is told."

<*This is one truth that I do not believe should be told.*> Subedi said. <*It can only cause... dissension and mistrust within the Collective. I am sure you agree with me, Ambassador Walid.*> Walid was silent as Subedi went on. <*I move we vote to suppress Truth-Finder Cray's report and deal with it as an internal matter.*>

I was going to tell Subedi that such a vote would be moot, as the truth inevitably comes out. Jebe intervened before I could.

<*The truth of this is already known. The members of my pod are in constant communication. What one has been told, all in the pod know – on this station, on our homeworld, and in our embassies.*> Jebe shrugged and let out what could only have been a sigh. <*Members of the council, the truth is out there.*>

This was news to all of us. I learned later that the other members of the Collective Council had not been aware that the Dagon seemed to have a group mind as well as individual ones. The truth of that was, as usual, a lot simpler.

There was nothing to say but, "Members of the Council, Loy will be giving you a list of the missing members of your races. I'm sure that you will wish to contact your governments regarding this matter as soon as possible. When you do, I would ask that you see if GenSeq records for those missing are available so we can identify our samples and give them whatever death rites are due. Let me take this time to emphasize that there is no evidence that Ambassador Walid was involved with or even knew about what Herat and others were doing.

"Members, this truth has been revealed and names have been named, I will leave the rest to you. Proceed as you will. Ambassador Walid, I surrender Bocaj to your custody. As for Loy and me, we still have the truth of Herat's death to discover. I remind you all of your interviews. Good day."

Chapter Ten

We had a few hours before the interviews started. Using the principle of getting the worst jobs over with, I scheduled Flandry first. He was to be followed by Del Caprine, Olubek, Walid, Subedi, and, finally, Jebe.

While we waited, Loy spent his time doing the grunt work that was dumped on all junior partners—tracing the sub-cuts of the missing sophonts, cataloging the evidence I'd processed, and identifying what still needed to be analyzed. (The vacuum samples for one. Nothing makes forensics more fun than literally sifting through dirt.) He was also trying to access Herat's computer. He had asked Omega Central for the passwords only to be told that, due to personal security issues, tablets are not connected to the station's cloud.

(Yes, there are clouds in space other than the Large and Small Meridionals. At least, my app translates large-sized communal data storage as a cloud.)

While Loy was about that, I was having my own "conversation" with Omega Central, trying to determine how difficult it would be to simulate someone's IMplant to gain access to their suite.

IN YOUR CAPACITY AS LEAD TRUTH-FINDER, YOU HAVE FULL ACCESS TO ANY AND ALL AREAS OF THE STATION, EVEN THOSE CONSIDERED PRIVATE.

Just what every cop dreams of, an open warrant to go anywhere. Wait until they hear about this on Terra, assuming I get back. Reports are that the Ackley Winds are stronger than ever.

"And if I were not Lead Truth-Finder, how would I gain access?"

IF YOU WERE NOT THE LEAD TRUTH-FINDER, YOU WOULD NOT BE ON THIS STATION AND SO YOUR QUERY IS MOOT.

I wasn't sure if I was asking the wrong question, if Omega was being very literal in the manner of all AIs, or if it had somehow become sophontic and was messing with me.

I decided I didn't want to know. It took me several rephrases before Omega finally informed me that if it were possible to copy another sophont's IMplant, the station would easily detect it and refuse to respond.

So, the short answer was that the killer had to have been given access to Herat's suite, admitted by Herat, or rushed in as he entered. The good news, most of the station staff was eliminated. The bad news, the possible suspects still included the ambassadorial staff.

All of whom had sub-cuts, which could be tracked.

"Loy, while you're tracking..."

I stopped when I discovered I was talking to myself, that Loy had left on an unknown errand.

He returned about fifteen minutes later, a notebook in his hand. It was a real notebook, not a digital one.

<*I went to Herat's quarters.*> (I had extended my access to him.) <*I found this in Herat's workroom. It was not very well hidden. It's all his passwords.*>

Of course. There are at least three universal constants — ceramic tile in communal bathrooms, meatballs in sauce (I think the Preada have a non-meat version), and the fact that very few sophonts can remember their passwords. You would think we'd store them in our IMplants, but no, we write them in a book and hide them someplace we think is safe but isn't.

Soon Loy had access and was ransacking Herat's personal files.

<*Most of this is business stuff. I found his downloads. Books — history, tech manuals, and religion. Music — classical, traditional, nothing popular. Videos — music performances, more history, investigative documentaries, and the like.*>

Loy started scrolling, opening this file and that. He eventually found a file he said was marked, "Consumers," or at least that's how my app translated it. At first, I thought it was a mistranslation of "Customers," but it turned out to be dead-on. It was a list of those to whom Herat had provided meat from the slaughtered members of Omega Station. No Preada, Anasi, or Dagon names were on it. Just Hunta, Karp, and Terran. I only recognized one name but that one was very interesting.

"These others will have to be checked to see if they were buying for themselves or someone higher up." Loy nodded that he understood. "Okay, copy that file and download it to our tablets for our reports."

<Copies to the Council?>

"Not yet."

<What about the rest of it?>

I knew what he meant by "rest of it."

"Hold the tablet for now. When we're done, we'll turn it over to Walid after warning her of its contents. Were you able to trace the missing?"

<I've traced most of them to Herat's suite then to a disposal chute.>

Again we were hit with the enormity of the slaughter. "At least we've named the dead. That's something."

<It's not enough. Friend Cray, Herat's death seemed well deserved. Do we have to find his killer?>

It was a good question. Justifiable homicide, unofficial justice, street law. Every cop had faced this question. The correct answer is always the same.

"Friend Loy, we are Truth-Finders. That's what we do. Our mission is not to decide whether Herat was deserving of death but to discover who killed him. If we fail, then the killer might decide some other sophont must die. We find them. It is up to others to decide their fate."

Loy gave a Hunta nod and sigh. <So what is next to do?>

"Trace the movements of the ambassadorial staff. See if…"

<I have already done that. None of the junior staff entered the Ambassadorial section. And the ambassadors themselves have special sub-cuts.>

"Which, I'm guessing, aren't trackable due to privilege." Loy nodded. "Okay, except for this name," I showed him which one, "cross reference the names on the consumers list to station personnel. We'll let the Council deal with them. Once you get the cross-referencing working, we'll rest, wash, eat, then start interviewing our suspects."

<I think there is one person we need to talk to first.>

When I thought about it, I had to agree.

Chapter Eleven

I decided to hold the interviews in the ambassadors' suites. Being "at home," as it were, would make them feel comfortable and give them a sense of security. With their guard down, they might say something they hadn't meant to.

Victor Flandry was not a gracious host. He did not offer us refreshments. Instead, he had an aide meet us at his door while he remained seated on the couch in the greeting area. Without waiting to be asked, I sat in a chair opposite. Loy made a point of moving the other chair and resting on his tail. From that position, he commanded the room, looking down at Flandry.

"Thank you for seeing us, Ambassador Flandry."

"I didn't seem to have a choice, so ask your damned questions and get out. This is Sheila Murphy. She will be sitting in on our interview and recording it."

Shelia Murphy was a brunette in her mid-thirties, about five-six with close-cut brunette hair. She was dressed in what seemed to be the station uniform—overalls (hers matched her hair) with an Omega patch on the left breast and a Terran United patch on both upper arms.

<Is she your legal advisor?> Loy asked.

"I would prefer that you and you alone address me, Detective Cray."

"Too damned bad. Answer Truth-Finder Loy's question."

"There are no alien Truth-Finders."

Okay, every race, every culture, has taboo words. Terra has quite a few of them. I mentioned one that the Hunta use to refer to the Preada. Ever since a Terran craft encountered one of the Karp's, the word "alien" has slowly worked its way into the taboo category. It suggests that the user feels superior to the race to which the word is directed. That they are "human" while the other race is less so. The word has gradually faded from use. Flandry's use of it could only have been a deliberate provocation. Why anyone would want to provoke a six-foot raptor with jaws that bite and claws that catch is beyond me. Still, Loy handled the insult well.

<Omega Station was not built for us. On it, we are all alien. And I am a Truth-Finder, albeit a junior one. My appointment by Adrian Cray has been registered with Terran Investigative Service. So again, please answer my question.>

"Ms. Murphy is my aide. I would normally have had my assistant Dominic Gray sit in, but I have not been able to contact him."

Loy and I knew why. We also knew more about Shelia Murphy than Flandry thought we did, thanks to our tracking of ambassadorial personnel. Murphy was a frequent visitor to Flandry's suite, apparently "aiding" him at all hours. I'll allow you to speculate on what she was aiding him with.

"Thank you, ambassador. I should however warn you that our questions will involve sensitive and delicate matters that you may wish to answer without witnesses present."

"Thank you for your warning, detective." The tone of Flandry's voice did not make him sound grateful. "You are recording this, are you not?"

"Yes, that was to be your next warning."

"Along with my rights?"

I just smiled. Damned fool thought Terra's rules still applied. Instead,

"To begin with, I'll need to scan your finger and palm prints and obtain a sample of your genetic sequence."

"So you can plant it on the crime scene. No, I don't think so."

Flandry's attitude and officiousness, along with his refusal to cooperate was getting on my nerves. Still, knowing what was coming, I continued to be pleasant, polite, and official.

"We've recovered and logged all the evidence from the crime scene. We're done with Herat's suite." (That's what I thought at the time, but more on that later.) "I purposely postponed the interviews and sample collections to avoid the possibility and suggestion that there may be cross-contamination. The samples are mainly to exclude you from consideration as a suspect." (As I've said, I lie about other things.)

Flandry thought about this for a moment. But he was that breed of sophont who, having made their stand, refused to back down from it.

"Nevertheless, I still refuse. I know my rights."

Loy and I had prepared for this. I nodded at him. "Loy?"

<*Omega, please explain to Terran Ambassador Flandry his rights concerning the investigation into Hunta Ambassador Herat's death. Include Aide Murphy in the explanation.*>

Omega's reply came through all our apps at the same time. I don't know about the others, but it still sounded like Omega was speaking in all caps.

OTHER THAN THOSE INHERENT IN AMBASSADORIAL PRIVILEGE, VICTOR FLANDRY DOES NOT HAVE THE RIGHT TO REFUSE TO BE QUESTIONED OR TO REFUSE TO PROVIDE EXCLUSIONARY AND/OR INCRIMINATING SAMPLES. SHOULD HE REFUSE THE LATTER, TRUTH-FINDERS CRAY AND/OR LOY MAY COMPEL HIM TO DO SO USING WHATEVER FORCE THEY DEEM NECESSARY.

Flandry paled, especially since Loy was looking at him with his mouth open and teeth bared. But he still seemed reluctant.

"Think about it, ambassador. Wouldn't it be easier to have me scan your fingers and palms and swab the inside of your cheeks than to have Loy knock you unconscious and then collect the samples?"

"Will you need samples from me as well?" Murphy asked. Her, I felt sorry for. This was all above her pay grade. She apparently had agreed to sit in on and record this interview as a favor for her boss (and whatever else he was to her). Now she was in a very tense situation that may devolve into violence. I wished I could warn her that things were only to get worse but instead I said,

"If you wish to provide them, Ms. Murphy. Maybe as an example to the ambassador, to show him there's nothing to it."

Murphy smiled and held up her fingers and palms for scanning. Then she opened her mouth wider than necessary to allow me to take the buccal swabs. When I was done, she put her hand on mine and whispered, "If you need anything else just let me know."

Not for the first time I asked myself if that was all anyone on Omega thought about. Then I wondered why *I* wasn't thinking about it. I put that down to my dedication to the task at hand.

Not wanting to be shamed in front of his aide, Flandry grudgingly gave us the needed sample.

"Thank you," I said as if he had been fully cooperative. "Now then, ambassador, I ask you again if you wish Shelia Murphy to remain for the interview?"

"Yes."

"Very well. For the record, you are Victor Flandry, the Terran Ambassador to the Collective Council on Omega Station?"

"Yes, I am."

"Did you kill, or cause to be killed, Herat, Hunta Ambassador to Collective Council on Omega Station?"

"No."

"Have you ever been inside Ambassador Herat's suite for any reason, either station-related or personal?"

"No."

Up until now, Flandry's short responses had been straightforward. His "Nos" had come promptly with no hesitation. My cop sense told me he was telling the truth. But just as I've lied before, I've also been wrong before. But he faltered on my next question.

"Do you know what a butchering room is?"

"Eh, no, eh, what's that?" The little quiver in his voice made me think he did. I didn't pursue it.

"Loy, if you would?" Loy had his tablet in a pouch that hung on a belt around his waist. He brought it out and displayed a pic.

"This is the knife found near Herat's body. Do you recognize it, either as yours or belonging to anyone with whom you're acquainted?"

"I, eh, it's a very common type of knife. I've seen the Karp wearing them." He paused as if deciding to tell us something. "I have one myself. Would you like me to get it for you?"

"No, thank you. Just tell Truth-Finder Loy where it is." It was in the top drawer of his nightstand. I wondered if Murphy could have told me that.

"Loy, would you please get the knife? And while you're at it, search for other knives like it."

"But he can't. Never mind, I guess he can." (Flandry was learning.)

"While Truth-Finder Loy conducts his search, would you tell me where you were and who you were with from the time the Collective Council meeting adjourned the day before Herat's body was found up to the finding of his body?"

"I, er, can't you get that information from Omega Central?"

"No, I can't. Your movements are protected by ambassadorial privilege. If, however, you want to waive that privilege for the duration of our investigation…"

"No, that would… set a bad precedent. What does it matter, since I've told you I didn't kill Herat?"

I gave him that one. "You're right, of course. We can revisit that if it becomes relevant."

Just then, Loy came back. He had a knife in his gloved hands.

<*Ambassador, is this your knife?*>

Flandry forced himself to look at Loy. "It is… detective."

<*I didn't find any others.*> Loy said as he handed the knife to me. I put on gloves and took it from him. I made a show of scanning it and swabbing the blade and hilt. Once I was done, I handed the knife to Flandry hilt first, to show him that I was not afraid of his being armed in my presence. He, in turn, placed the knife on the small table between us as if to say that he was not afraid of me either.

"Thank you, ambassador. We're almost done with the matter of Herat's death. But may I put a scenario to you?"

"Er, yes. Go ahead."

"We have evidence that the knife found by Herat's body was not the one that killed him. That it was deliberately planted by the killer to cast the blame on someone of a different race. There are other anomalies as well. Being from Terra, you are, of course, familiar with the tropes of mystery and crime fiction, one of those being the killer's framing of an innocent to get away with murder. What do you say to that?"

Flandry might have been officious pain-in-the-ass, but he was not stupid. He knew what I was implying. He rose from his seat.

"How dare you suggest that I would not only commit murder but plant evidence to incriminate…"

Say it, I thought, *say "an Anasi."*

But he continued with "someone else!"

"I didn't suggest anything. I merely wanted your opinion on a possible scenario that as a Terran you'd be familiar with. No matter. I'm done with questions about Herat's death."

"Thank the Lord."

"But there is one other matter. Loy, if you would? Ambassador Flandry, Ms. Murphy, please have a seat. We have something to show you."

Loy worked his tablet, and a Terran man appeared on the screen. It was Dominic Grimes, Flandry's assistant.

Chapter Twelve

Dominic Grimes was on Herat's list of "consumers." As Flandry's assistant, he might have been acting for the ambassador rather than consuming members of the other races himself. There was only one way to find out.

Using the warrant authority we had been granted, we decided to surprise Grimes, entering his suite without notice or knocking. Our surprise was complete, literally catching Grimes with his pants down, or rather, off.

When we requested entry, Omega advised us that Grimes was not alone. Not a problem, I had my shock rod and Loy had his claws. Loy and I began recording and entered.

There was no one in the greeting area but we could hear passionate noises coming from the bedroom.

<It would be impolite to interrupt them. Should we let them finish?>

I smiled at the idea but yelled out, "Dominic Grimes, this is Truth-Finder Cray. Get dressed and come out immediately."

From the bedroom, we heard shouts of surprise followed by "What the hell do they want?" and <Dommie, what did you do?> This last was in what my app told me was Preada.

Loy's app must have told him the same thing because he whispered, <This should be interesting.>

"You should hang back a bit. The Preada has already had one shock."

Loy agreed and moved to where he wouldn't immediately be seen by anyone coming from the bedroom.

The Preada came out first. She was dressed in a tunic and pants. Her fur was light tan and her mask dark brown. Grimes followed in a blue shirt and retro blue jeans.

"What the hell is this, Cray? Flandry warned us about you and your ways. You have no right…"

<We have every right.>

Loy's appearance was perfectly timed. The Preada let out a shriek. Grimes took a step back, stumbled, and almost fell.

<We weren't doing anything wrong.> The Preada said quickly in a soft and seductive voice that explained why she was doing it. As she protested, she cast nervous looks at Loy. Understandable, given the relationship between their races. <May I go?>

<Maybe she should stay?> Loy suggested.

"No, she should go," I said, hoping that she would never learn what this investigation was all about.

"Eh…"

<Elanda.>

"Yes, Elanda, Sorry to have interrupted you but we have urgent business with, eh, Dommie."

<Thank you.> Loy stepped aside as Elanda moved toward the door. But she stopped in front of him. <Would you please check to see if anyone's in the passageway?>

He did, there wasn't, and she was gone.

Grimes demonstrated that he was the perfect assistant to Flandry by shouting at us, "Now what the hell is this? Are you the morality police now? How dare you interrupt two consenting adults…"

I let him rant. When he paused to take a breath I said, "Dominic Grimes of Terra, I am placing you in custody for your complicity in the abduction and murder of at least thirty-two sophonts and possibly more, conspiracy to commit murder, and the receiving and devouring of sophontic flesh. You are relieved of all duties and will be confined to quarters. You will not be permitted to communicate with anyone except me and Truth-Finder Loy."

As I said this, Grimes's belligerent attitude faded, the blood rushed from his face, and he began quivering. He started muttering, "I knew it, I knew it, I knew it." Before I could ask him if he understood what I had told him, he broke down entirely.

"It was Flandry. He ordered me to do it, that is to pick up packages from that Hunta Bocaj."

"Where were the exchanges made?" I asked but by then he had collapsed in a chair and was sobbing.

Loy went over to Grimes and gently raised him to his feet.

<*I understand. Flandry was your commander and you had to do what he said.*>

"Yes, yes."

<*And you didn't know at first, did you?*>

"No."

<*But you suspected, didn't you? And there was talk…*>

"Yes, there was, and I did."

<*And you asked about it and…*>

"Flandry admitted it, and…"

<*Offered you a taste?*> Grimes nodded. <*Did he tell you what it was?*>

"He said, he said… it was Preada."

<*And that made it more exciting to mate with one of them, didn't it?*>

"Yes, God help me, yes."

Grimes collapsed and again started sobbing. Loy walked back to me.

"Very good," I said quietly. "You have a knack for this, Friend Loy."

Loy shrugged. <*I've always been good with others. What do we do with him?*>

We let Grimes cry it out. Then it was my turn. I went over and sat beside him.

"Mr. Grimes, we understand that Flandry put you in a very difficult situation, one you should not have been in. Even when you had a taste, it was because he told you to, right?"

Through the sobs came, "Ye… yes. Wha… what's going to happen to me?"

"That's not for us to decide. But you can help yourself by writing it all down. Everything Flandry or anyone else told you to do. What you did. Where you did it. What you know and what you heard."

"O…okay. I will."

I said to Loy. "Watch him. I'm going to search his quarters."

<*Do you think…*>

"Probably not, but following procedure is always a good idea."

Loy and I left him there, a sad, ruined man now all alone on a station many parsecs far from Terra. I would have felt sorry for him if he hadn't taken Elanda to his bed.

Ω

Flandry and Murphy watched the video I had taken of Grimes with resigned expressions. As soon as Grimes appeared on the scene they knew what he was going to say. When it was over, Murphy was the first to speak.

"I didn't know." Her protest came out in a pathetic squeak. "I mean, Victor never told me."

"Don't believe her," Flandry said, all his pretense and bluster gone. He was beaten and he knew it. It was time to salvage what he could. "She knew. She was in on it from the start. Eating one of the other races turned her on. We'd eat, hit the sack, and she'd go wild. When we walked through the station and Sheila would spot an Anansi, or a Karp, or a Preada, she'd giggle like a girl and whisper, 'We've eaten one of those.'"

"Victor's..."

Loy loomed over her. <Tell the truth, Ms. Murphy.>

Six feet of a feathered alpha predator can be quite intimidating so whatever she was going to say she didn't. Instead, she hung her head and admitted, "What he said. It's true. Damn me, it's true."

"What was your arrangement with Herat, Ambassador?"

Flandry shrugged. "What you'd expect. Credit for the product. Sometimes I'd vote the way he wanted in Council. Nothing that would hurt Terra, though. That's all."

"Tell the truth, Victor. Tell them or I will."

"A week before he was killed, Herat asked if I could get him a Terran, one that wouldn't be missed."

"And what did you tell him?"

Before Flandry could answer, Murphy said, "I don't know what Victor told him, but he asked me for a list of the station's Terran personnel and their duty assignments."

I left it there, stopping before Flandry said something that would make me take out my shock rod and use it until he stopped twitching. *Why not,* the nasty part of my mind asked. *You've got carte blanche. Indulge yourself.*

Instead, I fell back on procedure.

"Victor Flandry of Terra, I am detaining you for complicity in the abduction and murder of at least thirty sophonts and possibly more, conspiracy to commit murder, and the receiving and devouring of sophontic flesh. You are relieved of all duties and will be confined to quarters. You will not be permitted to communicate with anyone except me and Truth-Finder Loy."

I turned to Shelia Murphy. "Ms. Murphy, the same applies to you. Once we leave here, Truth-Finder Loy and I will escort you back to your quarters where you will be confined."

We left Flandry and locked up Murphy. When that was done…

<*Are you all right, Friend Cray?*>

"Right now, Friend Loy, I need to go look at the stars. After that, I think we'll go talk to Del Caprine."

Chapter Thirteen

Ambassador Del Caprine's quarters were not like the others I'd seen. Except for the bathroom and a small eating area, her suite was open space. There was a large cushion in what would have been the greeting area on which she reclined. Opposite that were several smaller cushions for the comfort of her guests, or discomfort depending on how easily one could get up and down. I had no problem. Loy didn't even try. He just leaned back on his tail.

When standing and with her upper thorax erect, the ambassador was slightly smaller than Loy and me. Her head was almost featureless, just a mouth and two round disks that served as sensory input. Her legs were thin and her body a mix of yellow and gray.

When the door to her quarters opened, Del Caprine chose to greet us, me really, with what had been an old joke between our races.

There was twittering, chirping, and clicking which my app translated as <Look out. It's a monster! Kill it!> This was accompanied by a certain tilt of her head which indicated laughing.

The proper response would have been for me to turn around, look for the monster, then realize she was referring to me. That was before the Anansi Affair.

Instead, I smiled, looked at Loy, and said, "It's just my partner, ambassador. Thank you for seeing us."

<As if I had a choice,> she said with another smile. <Please come in. Make yourselves as comfortable as possible.>

Once we were "as comfortable as possible," I said, "Ambassador, as you know, Truth-Finder Loy and I are conducting interviews concerning the murder of Ambassador Herat of the Hunta."

<I am not interested in finding his killer, Truth-Finder. After what you told the Council about his activities, his killer should go free. I am, however, interested in learning if you know any more about who else was involved in the trafficking of Anasi flesh.>

"We are working on both investigations, ambassador. Reports will be made to the Council when the time is right. For now, before we begin the interview, I have to ask if you will provide us with a sample of the adhesive that you use to hold objects and that of your venom."

A different twist of her head — wonderment, confusion — then, <I understand the adhesive, it contains my genetic sequences, but the... Ah, someone drugged Herat before slitting his throat. Yes, I could see how one of us would have to if we were to kill him. But it wasn't me. If it was, I would have done more. I would have butchered him as he butchered mine.>

"Another possibility is that, having learned about what Ambassador Herat was doing, you gained entry into his quarters, drugged him, and left the door unlocked. Once his absence was noticed, you returned to his quarters and slit his throat."

She was still for longer than I had expected her to be. When she did speak, the voice I heard in my app seemed flat and angry.

<I only wish that was true, Truth-Finder. But it is not. If I had, I would proudly announce it, protected as I am by my privilege.>

"I understand, ambassador, but I still need the samples."

Del Carine extended her arm and allowed me to take a swab of her adhesive. Then, in the presence of Loy and me, she opened her mouth and milked a fang.

"Thank you, ambassador."

Despite her denial, after securing the samples, I asked Del Caprine many of the same questions I had asked Flandry. She had not murdered him, did not know who did, and before finding his body, she had not been in his suite.

"So when you found the door opened and you saw him, you did not check on his well-being?"

<I saw no need. His throat was open, and he had bled out.>

"Or handle the knife that was found beside his body?"

<How could I if I was not in his suite? Oh, you found Anansi GenSeq on the knife?>

"I can't comment on any part of the investigation."

<If you did, and it is identified, I will use my privilege to protect her.>

When I didn't reply, Del Caprine added, <*It is a shame what happened between our two races.*> I allowed that it was. <*We overreacted and you underreacted. When I learned about your nuclear weapons I was, at first, appalled, then relieved that you did not use them on us.*> She held out a hand. I took it. <*Let us try to do better in the future.*>

"That's all any of us can do, ambassador."

Ω

Our last visit of the day was to Ambassador Olubek. He was small, even for a Preada; he was all black, body and mask, unusual for his kind. There was nothing unusual about the interview. Olubek greeted both of us politely, Loy more than me.

<*Let there be peace between us, my brother of Sauros.*>
<*For now and forever, brother. May the past be forgiven.*>
<*But never forgotten.*>

Samples were requested and freely given. Denials all around with an offer of the Preada version of sainthood for whoever did the deed. There was also a request to turn all those involved in sophont trafficking over to the Preada government.

"And what would your government do to them?" I asked.

<*There are airlocks. And the great nothing of the vacuum is cold and unforgiving.*>

I couldn't argue with that.

Chapter Fourteen

Despite searching, neither Loy nor I found any knives of the type recovered from Herat's suite in either Del Caprine's or Olubeck's suites. We made up for that in Subedi's quarters. Knives were displayed on two of the greeting area walls, eleven on the far wall, and another six on the right (outer) wall.

The suite itself was painted in primary colors, all brightness and light. The only dark spots were the knives on the wall.

I remember thinking that I might have my work cut out for me. (No pun intended.)

"Truth-Finder Cray," Subedi said in Terran. "How nice of you to come. I know that this is a formal visit but be welcomed as a guest. And welcome to you, Loy. What an honor it must be, to be the first non-Terran Truth-Finder. But not the last, I trust. Remember, in your position, you represent not only your race, but all the non-Terran races."

His voice was deep and carried a serious tone to it. He was dressed in what seemed to be business clothes — a medium blue shirt with a well-below-the-knees kilt of a darker blue. His face stripes and swirls were yellow mixed with orange. Seeing it tickled something in the back of my mind, but I didn't know what. I ignored it. If it was important it would come back. (I hoped.)

Subedi caught me looking, staring really.

"Thank the Great Mother for having us evolve on a planet that was mostly forest and jungle." He waved his hand at his face. "Camouflage was a survival trait. And yes, Truth-Finder, we are like this all over. I can show you if you like. The Great Mother made us as we are so why should we be ashamed."

"No thank you, ambassador." Loy declined as well.

Subedi spocked an eyebrow. "Mmm, very well. Some are curious about what the other races, well, you know." I did know, but this was neither the time nor place. And besides, he might want to look at me.

"Now then, as you are my guests and I am your host, let's drop the honorifics and use real names. And allow me to offer refreshments. Bread, vegetables, and meats from my home world. Also wine. Loy, does wine adversely affect you?"

<It does not. I think wine, along with beer, is one of those universal constants my partner is always speaking of.>

"When this is over, Adrian, we will have to talk about that. Now, let us eat and drink and talk."

As we ate, we discussed everything but the case, cases really.

<Subedi, I could not but notice how colorful your quarters are. Is that your own personal taste?>

"No, Loy, it is not. Most of us prefer bright colors. We were too long in the woods and jungles, having to hide from the beasts who hunted us and who we hunted in turn. The brightness reminds us that we no longer have to hide. Of course, there are fewer places to hide. We've cut down many of the trees to feed the great steam engines that power our industries and vehicles. We replant but demand always exceeds supply. How is it on Terra and Sauros?"

<Much the same as yours, at least for the Hunta. The Preada are much more connected with the land.> Loy let out a sigh. <One day we will work together, and both sides owe Karp a debt for forcing us to start.>

Subedi waved his hand as if to say, "One helps where one can."

"And, Adrian, how does Terra fare?"

"Well, thank you. Solar power, wind power, and wave power meet most of our needs."

"Mmm, maybe you're not the foolish, dangerous creatures everyone thinks you are. Well, at least not the foolish part."

We ate some more then emptied and refilled our glasses.

"Do you realize, Adrian, that the Karp and Terrans are the only two races that tell lies for entertainment?"

"How so, ambass... Subedi?"

"Fiction. We make up stories to amuse ourselves. Although yours is of a wider range than ours. You cover all aspects of life on Terra. We like extended sagas of war, love, physical encounters, and honor. Especially honor, whether is it taken, lost, or redeemed. Of course, duels and revenge always play a big part."

"You would probably enjoy the Terran authors Alexander Dumas Fils and Pere."

Subedi nodded thanks. "I will look into them."

<*I have heard of your honor duels, Subedi...*>

I knew where Loy was going and wondered if I should forestall him, but Subedi also knew.

"Yes, our honor duels. Like Terrans, we kill our own. But unlike them, and forgive me, Adrian, we kill only for honor, and never impulsively. We warn our targets that death is coming for them."

"You send them a knife, don't you, Subedi. Or you leave one where it will be found."

"Yes, Adrian, we do. Sometimes we tell them from whom it comes. Most times we don't."

<*So they know that death is coming, but not from who, where, or when?*>

"They may guess the who. This might lead them to figure out the where. As to the when, within five of our days."

"The knives on your wall are not purely decorative, are they, Subedi?"

"No, they are not. The knives on the wall behind me are ones that were left for me. Those who left them are gone. I am still here. I think that the reason I am on this station was that I was too good at meeting challenges. On the far wall are knives I have left and reclaimed or may one day leave. But that is all a matter for another time. Now, Adrian, I believe that you have questions for me."

Time to work. I started by requesting a scan of Subedi's ridge detail and a sample of his GenSeq. Subedi willingly complied.

"Subedi, how distinct are the Karp genetic sequences? Are your body markings genetically determined or are they random like Terran friction ridges?"

"An interesting question. I will ask one of our geneticists and get back to you. Although, since your work is mostly comparative, that is not immediately important, is it?"

No, it was just me being curious. I asked the standard questions and received the standard replies. Like Del Caprine and Olubek, Subedi declined to waive privilege to allow us to trace his movements. Like them, he mentioned not wanting to set a precedent.

<Subedi, do you recognize this?> Loy showed him a pic of the knife we recovered.

Subedi stood and made a show of looking at the knives hanging on his wall. Sitting down again, he said with a wry grin. "I may have seen knives like it."

"Is this one of yours?"

"No, it is not."

"Have you lost any knives, or have any been stolen?"

"No. Adrian, I know exactly where all my knives are."

"And when was the last time you cleaned them?"

"I clean them regularly as part of my religious practices. The last time was just before you arrived."

"May we photograph them, just for the record?"

"My understanding of your status is that you can do whatever you please but thank you for being polite."

I nodded at Loy who took photographs the way I had trained him to do—an overall of the room, a general shot of the knives on the wall, and section shots showing the individual knives.

<How are the knives affixed to the walls? I don't see any wires or hooks.>

Subedi seemed to hesitate before answering. When we returned to our quarters, I'd check the recordings we hadn't told him we were making.

"An adhesive the station's combined laboratories made. It is based on the Anasi's gripping adhesive." He sighed. "I suppose you want a sample. There are jars in my workroom. Feel free to take one. And to keep you from having to politely ask, yes, you may search the rest of my suite."

We took a jar of adhesive and searched the suite. Some of the things we found in the bedroom had us wondering but we didn't find any more knives. We thanked Subedi for his cooperation and hospitality and left.

Returning to our quarters, I said to Loy, "You didn't eat much, mostly bread and vegs. You mostly let the meat alone."

<I took some meat, chewed it, then wiped my face. The meat is in my napkin, which is in my pocket. I would like to find out if it belongs to any race I know.>

Chapter Fifteen

At Ambassador Jebe's request, I went to their suite alone. Loy didn't mind.

"Afraid?"

<*Of course not.*> Like me, my partner lied about other things. I think I may have been a bad influence on him. <*Remember what we were saying about staring into the Abyss? If the Abyss has a mortal form, it comes from Dagos. If Jebe and the rest are even mortal.*>

"I'll tell them that you regret not being able to come, but that you are looking forward to their next communion." Loy made a gesture that also seems to be a universal constant among sophonts who have fingers to give. "While I'm with Jebe, download and review the pics you took to see if anything stands out. And start the processing of the GenSeq samples and the touch point scans."

<*I'll get them running then look at the pics. Good luck with the Abyss.*>

No one greeted me when the door to Ambassador Jebe's quarters opened. I hesitated a moment as if someone might suddenly appear and bid me enter of my own free will. When no one did, I went in. The door closed behind me.

The suite was dark, not pitch dark, but there was only enough light to see for about five feet. From what the light from the corridor revealed, it appeared as if the interior walls had been removed so that the suite was one big room.

A voice came out of the darkness.

<*Forgive the lack of light, Truth-Finder. We live in the shadows, between the light and the dark. Ours is a twilight existence, in the zone between the burning of our sun and the coldness of space. There is a chair to your left, please be seated.*>

I had noticed the chair. As I sat, Jebe stepped into what light there was. For the first time, I saw a Dagon without their cloak and hood. They stood naked before me as if inviting me to examine them. So I did.

Jebe was taller than a Preada, but not as tall as me or a Hunta. Their hairless head seemed "normal" — mouth, ears, nose, eyes all in their usual positions, except that their eyes were large, very large. All the better to see in the dark, I guess. It was below the head that things got, well, weird.

Jebe had no shoulders, their arms seemed to come out of their torso. I call them "arms," but they were actually intertwined tentacles that separated where a wrist would be to become digits. The "legs" were similar, flexible, intertwined tentacles, so there was no need for knees or elbows. The legs did not separate but rather flattened and there was a slight squelch when Jebe moved, the suckers adhering to the surface then pulling away.

Jebe's torso was round and smooth. No tentacles, no nipples, no genitals. The obvious question must have been plain on my face because Jebe said,

<We embrace and wrap our limbs around each other. There are often more than two of us. We take each other's essence into ourselves, and the next generation is part of us all. Other races can share as well, their essence becoming part of us.>

Not sure if that was an invitation or not, all I said was, "Like the snallygasters on Terra."

Jebe sounded surprised. <You have creatures like us on your home planet? Are they... aware?>

"I don't know. I know they exist. There are reliable records from our twentieth century. But few have seen them. They are elusive, and secretive."

<As are we.> Jebe said as their lower limbs collapsed until we were eye to eye. <Have you noticed, Truth-Finder, that there is no night anywhere on the station? Expect in our quarters, and perhaps when you and the others sleep, the lights are on all the time. That is why we cover ourselves. Not only to hide our true shape from the other races but to hide from the light.>

That was good to know. If I ever had to fight a Dagon, my weapon would be a 200K lumen flashlight. As for the Dagon's true form, I wondered if it was the one Jebe was showing me.

<I know you have questions, Truth-Finder, but I would like to ask some of my own.>

Why not? This was my last interview. When it was over I had to start figuring things out. Might as well delay the difficult task for as long as possible.

"Go ahead."

<*The word Terrans use for my planet? Where does it come from?*>

"The first Terran to encounter your race was a fan of a writer from the early twentieth century, a man named Lovecraft. The man wrote of weird creatures from other worlds and dimensions, of old gods that were banished from Terra. These gods and creatures had strange names. He called your race "Dagon" and your planet 'Dagos.' There was a more descriptive name. but few people could spell it."

<*I have paused my translation app. Please say the name no one can spell.*>

"Cthulhu."

Jebe's tentacles shuddered.

<*Please pause your app.*> When I did I heard Jebe say, < *Cthulhu*> When I unpaused my app they added, <*In our language that is a cry for help.*>

And I thought things were weird before.

<*I shall have to read this Lovecraft. Between him and the snallygaster, perhaps our people are closer than we imagine. But please, ask your questions.*>

I asked for samples. Jebe allowed me to swab their mouth. Given the number of tentacles and the number of suckers on each, I settled for scanning some of the suckers on one limb as a matter of procedure since I hadn't found any on the scene.

I asked my questions, Jebe answered them all in the negative. But they would allow our tracking of their movements.

"I have one more question, ambassador. If the Dagon are as connected as you said at the meeting, why did you not notice that some of them were missing?"

My app indicated that the sounds Jebe was making were chuckling.

<*It seemed you needed help, so I helped. It has been my experience that even intelligent sophonts will believe anything.*>

Including certain Truth-Finders.

"Ambassador, I must conduct a search of your quarters for knives or anything else that might be connected to the killing of Herat."

<*Do what you must. I will turn away. Just keep your light away from me.*>

I searched. I may have missed something. I may have missed a lot of things. I did the best that I could but came up empty.

<It has been interesting, Truth-Finder. Before you go, I have a request.> I nodded a "Go ahead." <When your investigations are over, please turn the ones who killed the others to us.>

"None of your kind was taken."

<Those on this station have become our kind. You are my kind. I will not see my kind killed and eaten.>

"That will be for the Collective Council to decide. And you are a part of that council."

<Indeed I am. Thank you, Truth-Finder. I must now see if this Lovecraft is in the station audio library.>

The preliminaries were over. But when I left Jebe's quarters I was not thinking of the real work ahead of me but of H. P. Lovecraft and if what he wrote was really fiction.

Chapter Sixteen

While Loy worked quietly behind me, I reviewed what we had. A lot of facts and speculation. Most of it was probably useless. But how to tell the good stuff from the bad? However, that was the job and if it was easy anyone could do it. And then where would I be? Probably back in the Sol System enjoying myself.

I downloaded the interviews to my tablet. I think better when I see things on a screen rather than in my head. Someone was lying, but who? And what was it about the color yellow? I didn't know. When in doubt, go back to start.

I pulled up the video and photographs of the crime scene. Went over them room by room, frame by frame, and pic by pic. Did I miss something? Kitchen—no. Bathroom—no. Well, maybe a swab or two but that's not where the murder occurred. Or was it? No drag marks, no green blood drops forming a trail on the yellow rug. (Yellow?) Sleeping area—if Herat had been mammalian he would have had a bed, and there would be sheets and pillows to recover to examine for hairs (feathers), fibers, and GenSeqs. I had found feathers (Herat's) and fibers but nothing that cried out, "Behold the Sophont!" The Greeting Area—the space where Herat fell. The knife, which was probably not THE KNIFE, the pool of green blood the knife was found in.

No, I had done everything I could. So what, if anything, did I miss? The suite had been done and dusted, all the evidence found and collected. I had even taken a sample from the pool of blood, even though I knew it to be Herat's. Yes, I had done everything.

Then it hit me. Maybe a small oversight that usually meant nothing. I had sampled Herat's blood but had not searched the blood.

Crime scene investigators call it "stirring the soup." You find a pool of fresh blood on a crime scene, and you take a stick and carefully swish it around to see if there's anything hidden in the blood. Most of the time it's bullets from the shooter standing over the victim and firing a few "just to be sure" shots. Once there was a collectible coin the assailant had dropped just before doing the deed. The CSI found it in the blood and traced it to the killer.

Only Herat's blood was dried, not fresh. Maybe that's why I missed it.

<Friend Cray, I've found...>

"Tell me later. Right now we have to go back to the crime scene."

Except for Loy having removed Herat's personal papers, everything was still as I had left it. Masked and gloved with scalpel in hand, I knelt down as if in prayer and began to scrape, a little at a time, taking off layer after layer like the universe's best archeologist.

I don't know how long I was there. There is no time on crime scenes. I do know it was long enough for my back to start aching. At one point I heard Loy say, <While you're down let me tell you...>

"Not now," I said. "Whatever it is, it can wait until I at least stand up. If I can stand up." (Loy told me that I had shouted. As I probably had, I took him at his word and apologized. When he finally told me what he had found, I apologized again.)

I scraped and scraped, long enough to think I was on a fool's errand. Then, I saw what looked like a small piece of the yellow carpet. But I wasn't down to floor level yet. I scraped some more, concentrating on the yellow. Finally, when what it was became clear, I stopped long enough for Loy to take a pic.

<Friend Cray, is that a...>

"I believe it is, Friend Loy."

I stopped scraping, started cutting it free of the dried blood, finally removing it with tweezers. I had Loy take another pic, to show that there was still blood underneath.

With Loy's help, I stood and held up my find, a yellow feather that had been left on the scene while the crime was in progress.

<So, Ambassador Walid?>

"Yes."

<How do we prove she was there? Someone could have planted it, as they did with the knife.>

"I have an idea about that. Omega?"

YES. TRUTHFINDER?

"Please track Ambassador Walid's movements on the day Herat was found."

I CANNOT COMPLY. WALID OF SAUROS IS PROTECTED BY AMBASSADORIAL PRIVILEGE.

"Walid of Sauros was not an ambassador until the day after Herat was found. Please track her movements up until her appointment."

At first, I thought Omega was going to refuse on the basis that privilege was retroactive. But instead…

DOWNLOADING TO YOUR AND TRUTHFINDER LOY'S IMPLANTS.

And there she was, entering Herat's suite an hour before Del Caprine found his body.

ANYTHING ELSE, TRUTHFINDER?

"Yes, as soon as you can, lock Ambassador Walid in her quarters and cut off communications with everyone except me and Loy."

SHE IS THERE NOW. LOCK DOWN INITIATED AND COMPLETE.

"Thank you, Omega."

<But, Friend Cray, Hunta do not kill each other.>

"I know. That means she had help. And I'm willing to bet you have a good idea who it was."

<Yes, I do. But first, Omega has finished tracing the missing. The last records of the ones for whom we could not account show they were in or near the Chief of Maintenance's office.>

"Looks like Ivalie has some explaining to do. At least we know why she sic'd her goons on us."

I queried Omega about Ivalie and was told she was in her quarters. "Does she share with anyone?"

HER POSITION PROVIDES HER WITH QUARTERS TO HERSELF. SHE IS CURRENTLY ALONE.

"Lock her down. Same restrictions."

<What about her, as you called them, goons?>

"We know who they are. We can find them if we need to. What else do you have?"

<I reviewed the pics I took in Subedi's quarters. At first, all seemed normal, but do you remember my asking him how he attached the knives to the wall?>
I nodded. < Their arrangement seemed odd. There were six knives on one wall, trophies of Subedi surviving a challenge. Very neat, two rows of three. On the other wall there were eleven, two rows of four, the bottom one of three.>

"And?"

<What if there had been twelve? And the twelfth knife is the one you recovered, the one the evidence suggests was not used to kill Herat. Perhaps it was not left behind to incriminate someone else, but a knife Subedi sent to Herat to mark a challenge?>

"How would he deliver it?" I asked, then answered myself. "He gave it to Walid, to be left in Herat's suite. Once the knife was delivered and the warning given, Subedi would feel justified in killing Herat. And that's why you asked about how he attached them to the wall."

<I enlarged the pics I took. If there had been twelve knives, Subedi would have had to adjust one row, centering three of them. I enlarged the close-up pics. See here.>

Loy brought up the close-ups on his tablet, zoomed in on the bottom row of three knives. <There are smudges on either side of the row and between the knives. Possibly adhesive from where the knives were. Adhesive from the jar we recovered is a match for that found on the knife.>

"He knew it would be. He also knew we'd find the jar and recover it, so he volunteered it."

<Proof enough for a lock down?>

"Maybe, but there are other jars out there. We'd have to test quite a few to show this jar was unique. But you have more, don't you?"

We'd only been together for a short time, but I'd come to know my partner. He got jittery when excited.

<Yes, I do. And I am very glad that I only chewed the meat Subedi offered us then spat it out. It did belong to a race we know.> Loy paused for effect, then hit me with it. <I had it analyzed. It was Karp.>

What was it Bocaj said? <Sometimes, he'd feed them their own and tell them it was some other race.>

Subedi probably fed us the meat as a private joke. Maybe he knew it was Karp, maybe he didn't. Maybe he didn't care if we found out. Ambassadorial privilege and all that. But if he didn't know, why the challenge?

"He knew, Loy, he knew it was Karp meat and he fed it to us as a sick joke."

<Why do you say that?>

"He was part of it. The only way he would have issued a challenge to Herat was if he found out that he had been served the meat of his own race."

<How would he have known? He probably would not have recognized the taste of Karp.>

I thought about this. There was only one answer.

"Walid knew. Either Herat told her, or she found something on his tablet, or maybe Bocaj informed her, either as payback for his demotion or he was still working for Herat in procurement. If the last, he might have assumed she was in on it and said something. So she told Subedi, and he enlisted her help."

<What does she get out of it?>

"She rights a great wrong and at the same time winds up on the council."

<But she said she didn't want the post. Ah, she said she didn't want it. But maybe she did.>

"We'll have to ask her, about that and Bocaj. She's been isolated for a while now. Maybe she's ready to talk. The truth is her only way out. She was never involved in sophont trafficking. When she did find out, she consulted a member of the council who convinced her to help him with his challenge. Who knows, maybe she'll come out of this a hero. Meanwhile,

"Omega, lock down Ambassador Subedi's suite."

YES, TRUTHFINDER, AS SOON AS HE ARRIVES.

"Thank you, Omega."

A thought suddenly occurred to me. "Loy, when you chewed the meat, did you pretend to swallow before using the napkin?"

<No, I did not.>

"Subedi knows, Loy. Knows that you obtained a sample and that we would analyze it and learn the truth. That's why he answered my questions about the knife and his knives the way he did. He knows. He also knows there is only one way out for him."

<What is that?>

"Remember his walls. Subedi is all about honor. With him knowing what we know, he would see only one honorable end to this."

Chapter Seventeen

It was Subedi who made the first move. Omega advised me that a Karp representing Subedi was requesting entry. I advised Omega to allow it.

She was young, a very junior aide perhaps, with brown and tan markings. She carried a cross-body bag and was wearing a white shirt and blue trousers. She had probably heard all the stories and rumors about dangerous Terrans and fierce Hunta. She entered my quarters timidly, a frightened child sent into the monsters' den, not knowing if she'd come out alive.

She started as the door closed behind her and Loy instantly went into his gentle, comforting mode. Slowly approaching her, he extended an arm, saying <Welcome. My name is Loy. My partner's name is Cray. What is your name?>

<I... I am Lorac.>

<We mean you no harm, Lorac.> She didn't seem to believe him, not even when he added, <Enter freely and leave in peace. Please, have a seat.>

I stood by a chair, leaving Lorac the couch. But she declined Loy's invitation. <Thank you but no. I have come from Ambassador Subedi.>

<And where is the ambassador?>

Lorac's eyes were on me as she answered Loy.

She hesitated, unsure what to say, how much to give away. I took a guess.

"He came to your quarters, didn't he?"

<Y...yes. But he is not there now. He gave me a gift and a message to give to you.>

Lorac reached into her bag. Loy stiffened and I prepared to duck and dodge. But all she did was take out a sheathed knife, which was both a gift and a message. She walked over and handed it to me.

<You understand?>

"I do. Should you see the ambassador, please tell him that I await his pleasure, and will not be hard to find."

<Thank you. May I, may I go now?>

"Yes, you may. Loy?"

Loy opened the door and Lorac all but ran from my suite. After she left Loy said,

<An attractive young female, if you like mammals. What do you think?>

"About Lorac or about this?" I held up the knife.

<Both, and should I have Omega track her?>

"I'm guessing that there's one less knife on Subedi's wall. As for Lorac, yes, she is attractive. And no, don't track her. I think that might be cheating. Let the challenger find us."

<We should be on guard. Will you be taking your shock rod?>

"Loy, I'm a cop from Terra. I have more than one weapon. Now, let's go for a walk."

With Loy in his uniform black tunic and kilt and me in my red shirt, black cargo pants, and black jacket, he and I began a leisurely stroll around the top level of Omega. I found myself thinking of the old twentieth-century Western videos. Long forgotten, they were revived for a new audience about thirty years ago. Two gunslingers facing each other on a dusty street, knowing only one would walk away. There would tension in the air and suspenseful music playing in the background. Foolishly, I wished had on boots with spurs and a six-shooter on my hip.

We were in a passageway near the council room when…

<He's behind us.> Loy whispered, not turning around.

I didn't turn either as I asked, "How do you know?"

<Hunta's have a keen sense of smell.>

"I didn't know that."

<You never asked.>

We turned just as Subedi began his charge. His knife was in his right hand, the blade up for a disemboweling stroke. The knife he'd given me was strapped to my side. I left it there. If he thought this was going to be a gentlemen's duel, my knife against his, he was wrong. I wasn't a gentleman, I was a cop and as I told Loy, I had more than one weapon.

I let Subedi get closer then pulled my slug-thrower from my jacket pocket and put a bullet through his left eye. He died right away, his momentum carrying him a few more feet before he collapsed. My pistol was air-powered so there was no noise to attract a crowd. The only witnesses were Loy and Lorac, who was some distance back. On seeing Subedi fall, she came forward, looked over the body, and said, <He died as he would have liked, with his knife in his hand and an enemy in front of him. He died with honor.>

I didn't see it that way. There's no honor in death and no honor in killing. But then I'm a cop, not a Karp.

<Subedi left me with one last message for you.>

"What is it?"

<Thank you.>

Chapter Eighteen

Herat's death was not the end of things. At the request of those members of the Collective Council who weren't dead or under lockdown (Olubek, Jebe, and Del Caprine), Loy and I located and detained the others Herat's notes identified as "consumers." Most were his fellow Hunta but there was also a Terran lab manager in the comparative biology research laboratory. She claimed it was the only way she could get certain samples. No one believed her and none of her co-workers supported her story. Another was a Karp who made FTL flights between the station, the Karp homeworld, and its colonies.

<*I always thought there was something suspicious about him,*> my friend Exios said one night. (As it turned out, he did like dangerous, Terran males who stood six-foot tall.)

Another request was that after the whole affair was over, I remained to create and train a "peacekeeping unit" that would "investigate problems and situations that threatened the safety of the station and those within it." My first decision was to put Loy in charge of it and task him to recruit and vet a team that would include members of all races. My second was to establish a Forensics Lab.

There were other smaller tasks, all of which could have been delayed but weren't as a means of ignoring the elephant in the room.

As the more or less ranking members of our race, Loy and I were often invited to the council meetings as non-voting consultants. The governments of Terra, Hunta, and Karp were waiting to see who else on the station was implicated before deciding whether to promote from within or send someone new.

It was at a meeting held to discuss the problem that had been tabled when Herat's death was discovered — that of the Ackley Winds and whether to build larger FTLs.

"Has anyone suggested using sails?" I asked. I could tell from the way they reacted that no one had.

"All of our home planets have oceans or large bodies of water."

<Dagos does not,> Jebe corrected. <What there were in the times before the asteroid strike either froze or boiled away. But in the shadows in which we dwell there are some sizable lakes that are navigable.>

"Thank you, Jebe. Instead of fighting against the winds why don't we harness them? It would take time to develop and, yes, we may lose some ships and the AIs who pilot them, but in the end, the benefits might outweigh the losses."

From their actions, I could tell the idea impressed them.

<We would never have thought of that,> Olubek commented. <Thank you, Cray.>

<That's why he's the Truth-Finder> Loy responded. <By the way, Friend Cray, what am I now?>

"Chief of Police, pending approval of the full council."

<For now, we are the full council,> Jebe said. <And Chief Loy has our approval. And, Cray, two of our pod have shed tentacles. Communion and sharing will be in three days. You are invited to attend.>

"Is sharing what I think it is?"

<Yes, you will do us honor if you add your essence to our pod.>

"The honor will be mine. But for now, members of the council, there's one other thing to discuss, the most important thing. Punishment for those involved in sophont trafficking and justice for their victims."

<What do you suggest, Truth-Finder Cray?> Del Caprine asked.

I was sure that the Council had already made its decision. What they didn't know was that I had made some plans of my own.

"Members of the Collective Council, I said that once you knew the truth, the decision would be in your hands. But let me point out that Ambassador Walid had no part in the trafficking but instead did what she thought best to stop it."

<She participated in the death of one of her race and hid the truth, a truth she could have revealed at any of the council meetings she attended.>

"I would suggest, Ambassador Olubek, that she does not deserve the same fate as the others."

<Anyone else, Truth-Finder Cray? The Terran Grimes perhaps?>

"If he hadn't eaten the meat, Ambassador Del Caprine, and hadn't had sex with the Preada Elanda, I'd argue that his actions were coerced. As it is, he's guilty but like Walid, not as guilty as the others."

Jebe spoke up. <Olubek, your race was the most sinned against, not just on the station but on your homeworld. If Del Caprine agrees, we leave the fate of these two in your hands.>

Olubek gave a deep sigh, one I had heard under other, more pleasant circumstances, then shook his head. <They are all guilty, the degree of guilt does not matter.>

I could have argued that, as an ambassador, Walid had immunity for her actions. But her actions were taken before her promotion. My argument could only benefit Flandry. Besides, the issue was moot.

I shook my head to let the council know I had nothing.

<Very well,> Jebe said. <Olubek, Del Caprine, shall it be as we discussed?>

<It shall,> they both replied.

<Omega Station, this is Jebe of Dagos, speaking with the authority of the Collective Council. Please stop all life support of those under lockdown and advise when life signs have stopped.>

VERY WELL. There was a pause then, AMBASSADOR WALID IS NOT IN HER QUARTERS

<Locate her!>

AMBASSADOR WALID IS NO LONGER ON OMEGA STATION

Of course, they looked at me. I gave them my best cop stare and said, "I suspected your decision had already been made. So this morning, I had Omega release Walid into my custody. Right now she's on a FTL en route to Sauros."

<You had no right!> Olubek was not pleased. Del Caprine didn't seem to care. As for Jebe, like I said before, who can tell with a Dagon.

I answered with a shrug. Maybe I didn't have the right, but Omega had allowed it and that was good enough for me.

LIFE SUPPORT IN THE LOCKED DOWN AREAS HAS BEEN SHUT OFF. MONITORING LIFE SIGNS.

The meeting broke up. There was no need to wait. Theirs would be a slow, painful death. A warning message to others.

Epilogue

I communed and shared with Jebe's pod. Having done so, I am now an "honored one" of Dagos as a small part of me will forever be a part of them. Once Loy's team was trained and the Crime Lab working and approved, it was time for me to leave. I had one last dinner with Loy, one last night with Exios, and one last look at the stars.

I left Omega Station wondering if I'd ever return. When I did, I hoped to go sailing among the stars.

About the Author

JOHN L. FRENCH is a retired crime scene supervisor with forty years' experience. He has seen more than his share of murders, shootings, and serious assaults. As a break from the realities of his job, he started writing science fiction, pulp, horror, fantasy, and, of course, crime fiction.

John's first story "Past Sins" was published in Hardboiled Magazine and was cited as one of the best Hardboiled stories of 1993. More crime fiction followed, appearing in Alfred Hitchcock's Mystery Magazine, the Fading Shadows magazines, and in collections by Barnes and Noble. Association with writers like James Chambers and the late, great C.J. Henderson led him to try horror fiction and to a still growing fascination with zombies and other undead things. His first horror story "The Right Solution" appeared in Marietta Publishing's *Lin Carter's Anton Zarnak*. Other horror stories followed in anthologies such as *The Dead Walk* and *Dark Furies*, both published by Die Monster Die Books. It was in *Dark Furies* that his character Bianca Jones made her literary debut in "21 Doors," a story based on an old Baltimore legend and a creepy game his daughter used to play with her friends.

John's first book was *The Devil of Harbor City*, a novel done in the old pulp style. *Past Sins* and *Here There Be Monsters* followed. John was also the consulting editor for Chelsea House's *Criminal Investigation* series. His other books include *The Assassins' Ball* (written with Patrick Thomas), *Souls on Fire, The Nightmare Strikes, Monsters Among Us, The Last Redhead, the Magic of Simon Tombs, The Santa Heist* (written with Patrick Thomas), *In the Ruins of Caerleon, Daylight Comes*, and *The Wages of Syn*. John is the editor of *To Hell in a Fast Car, Mermaids 13,* C. J. Henderson's *Challenge of the Unknown, Camelot 13* (with Patrick

Thomas), *With Great Power...* (with Greg Schauer) and (with Danielle Ackley-McPhail) *Devilish and Divine* and *Grease Monkeys*.

You can find John on Facebook or you can email him at jfrenchfam@aol.com.

www.ingramcontent.com/pod-product-compliance
Ingram Content Group UK Ltd.
Pitfield, Milton Keynes, MK11 3LW, UK
UKHW040734200225
455358UK00001B/63